P9-DNA-290

almost identical

two-faced

by Lin Oliver

Grosset & Dunlap
An Imprint of Penguin Group (USA) Inc.

GROSSET & DUNLAP
Published by the Penguin Group
Penguin Group (USA) Inc., 375 Hudson Street, New York, New York 10014, USA
Penguin Group (Canada), 90 Eglinton Avenue East, Suite 700,
Toronto, Ontario M4P 2Y3, Canada
(a division of Pearson Penguin Canada Inc.)
Penguin Books Ltd., 80 Strand, London WC2R 0RL, England
Penguin Group Ireland, 25 St. Stephen's Green, Dublin 2, Ireland
(a division of Penguin Books Ltd.)
Penguin Group (Australia), 250 Camberwell Road, Camberwell, Victoria 3124, Australia
(a division of Pearson Australia Group Pty. Ltd.)
Penguin Books India Pvt. Ltd., 11 Community Centre,
Panchsheel Park, New Delhi—110 017, India
Penguin Group (NZ), 67 Apollo Drive, Rosedale, Auckland 0632, New Zealand
(a division of Pearson New Zealand Ltd.)
Penguin Books (South Africa) (Pty.) Ltd., 24 Sturdee Avenue,
Rosebank, Johannesburg 2196, South Africa

Penguin Books Ltd., Registered Offices: 80 Strand, London WC2R 0RL, England

If you purchased this book without a cover, you should be aware that this book is stolen
property. It was reported as "unsold and destroyed" to the publisher, and neither the author nor
the publisher has received any payment for this "stripped book."

All rights reserved. No part of this book may be reproduced, scanned, or distributed in any
printed or electronic form without permission. Please do not participate in or encourage piracy
of copyrighted materials in violation of the author's rights. Purchase only authorized editions.

Text copyright © 2012 by Lin Oliver. All rights reserved. Published by Grosset & Dunlap,
a division of Penguin Young Readers Group, 345 Hudson Street, New York, New York 10014.
GROSSET & DUNLAP is a trademark of Penguin Group (USA) Inc. Printed in the U.S.A.

Library of Congress Control Number: 2012007584

ISBN 978-0-448-45192-3 (pbk)   10 9 8 7 6 5 4 3 2 1
ISBN 978-0-448-49559-0 (hc)   10 9 8 7 6 5 4 3 2 1

ALWAYS LEARNING   **PEARSON**

For Sarah Baker ...
how lucky for us that you are the
first girl in our family—LO

The Invitation

························

Chapter 1

"Hey, Charlie," my brother, Ryan, said as he barged into me and my sister's room without knocking, something he's become very expert at. "Mail for you."

He held out a fancy-looking, navy-blue envelope with gold lettering on it. I don't get much mail, and I've certainly never gotten anything with my name and address in sparkly gold letters on it, so I instantly sprang off the bed, where I had been studying for my history midterm, and grabbed the envelope. Ryan, annoying person that he is, raised his arm high above his head and dangled the envelope in the air where I couldn't reach it.

"You're an aspiring cheerleader, Charles," he teased. "Let me see you jump for it."

Then, for no apparent reason, he started strutting

around my room like a chicken, flapping the envelope like it was a wing.

I don't know if you happen to have a fourteen-year-old brother or not, but if you do, I hope he doesn't act like a total jerk. Mine does most of the time. It's a mystery to me why so many girls think he's cool. As far as I'm concerned, my brother, Ryan, is seriously immature. I mean, why else would he parade around my bedroom waving an envelope and doing a chicken walk?

If Lauren Wadsworth could see him now, I thought, I bet her crush on him would disappear immediately, if not sooner.

"Ryan, could you grow up for a change and just give me the envelope?" I sighed.

"No way. Where's the fun in that?"

"It's mail, Ry. From the US Postal Service. It isn't supposed to be fun."

"See, that's your problem right there, Charles. You take life too seriously. It's not all about getting a good grade on your little history test."

That did it. The one thing I didn't need was academic advice from my "I think a C-minus is a perfectly fine grade" brother. With one swift leap, I lunged at him like a puma, snatching the envelope from his flapping hand.

"Nice move." He nodded approvingly. Ryan is a champion volleyball player and all-around great athlete, so he can appreciate a puma-like leap when he sees one.

I held the envelope in my hands and took a moment to study it. The paper was a dark, rich blue and soft as velvet. My name and address were spelled out in beautiful gold calligraphy. Ms. CHARLOTTE JOY DIAMOND, it said. Usually, I hate being called Charlotte, which is my full name. Everyone has called me Charlie from the moment I was born, just like we call my identical twin sister Sammie, even though her real name is Samantha Ellen Diamond. But when I saw my whole name written out in that elegant handwriting and sparkling like jewelry, I felt like it was the most beautiful name in the world.

Ryan was hanging over my shoulder, sticking his nose into what was clearly my business.

"Smell the envelope," he said. "You won't believe it."

Okay, now he had officially lost his mind.

"Unlike you, I don't sniff envelopes," I told him.

"Well, then you're totally missing out, Charles, because it smells like peanuts. No kidding."

"Yeah, right," I said. But my curiosity got the best of me, and I confess, I took a quick whiff. Amazingly, Ryan was right. There was a distinct smell of salty peanuts.

I stuck my finger under the flap and ripped it open, and an even stronger aroma of peanuts wafted out. I pulled out what looked like an invitation, and my eyes nearly popped out of my head. This sure wasn't the usual card with balloons or glitter or party hats that invites you for pizza and mini golf. This was the mother of all invitations. On the front cover it said, YOU ARE INVITED TO ATTEND THE BAR MITZVAH OF BENJAMIN AARON FELDMAN ON SATURDAY, NOVEMBER 23, AT TEMPLE BETH HILLEL. That part seemed pretty normal. But when I opened it up, a life-sized paper baseball popped up and stared me in the face. I swear it must have been sprayed with peanut scent, because it smelled just like those red-and-white-striped bags of peanuts you get at the baseball stadium. And get ready for this: In big, gold printing spread out across the baseball, it said, THE CELEBRATION CONTINUES AT DODGER STADIUM WITH AN ALL-STAR PARTY IN THE CLUB HOUSE. DINNER, DANCING, A PRIVATE LOCKER ROOM TOUR, AND AMUSEMENTS GALORE!

"Dodger Stadium." Ryan whistled. "That Feldman knows how to throw a party."

"This isn't happening," I answered. "Who rents out an entire baseball stadium?"

"The Feldmans do, that's who. Ben Feldman's family is rolling in money. They build airplanes or boats or rockets or something. I hear their house has fourteen bedrooms."

"That's ridiculous, Ryan. Who told you that?"

"Lauren. And she should know. Her parents have been best friends with the Feldmans since, like, forever."

That figured. The Wadsworths and the Feldmans were two of the forty families who own the Sporty

Forty beach club. It's their private club sitting right smack on the best beach in all of Santa Monica, with two tennis courts and cushioned lounge chairs and red umbrellas and a giant redwood deck for sunset barbecues. I happen to know the club well, because we live there. Not that we're rich or anything, although, I wouldn't mind it if we were. We're definitely not one of the Sporty Forty families. My dad was hired by Chip Wadsworth as the tennis coach for the club, and Ryan, Sammie, my dad, and I are living in the caretaker's apartment for a year while my mom is away at cooking school. Hopefully, when she comes back, we'll be able to move out and she'll start a restaurant.

The kids of the Sporty Forty families have all grown up together and are really tight. They call themselves the SF2s. Ben Feldman is one of them. And Lauren Wadsworth is basically their unofficial leader.

Oh, and did I tell you, she's my new best friend? At least, I hope she is.

Since Sammie and I had just transferred to Beachside Middle School, I was truly surprised and thrilled to get the invitation to Ben Feldman's bar mitzvah and party. We just started at this school this year, and I didn't think we'd made the SF2 invite list yet. Obviously, Ryan was surprised, too.

"Well, somebody's moving up in the world," he said. "Looks like my little sister Charlie has friends in high places."

"Didn't you get invited?" I asked him.

"Of course I'm invited. Check me out—who wouldn't invite this hunk? Not sure I'm going, though. I'm in eighth grade, little one. We think twice about going to parties with seventh-graders."

"If seventh-graders are so terrible, then how come you're going out with Lauren Wadsworth, who, last time I checked, is in seventh grade?"

"First of all, we are not going out. She happens to like me, which is understandable given my fabulous bod and awesome personality."

He stopped talking and kissed his bicep. Not kidding. He really did that.

"And second of all, I am a friendly type of guy who happens to appreciate beauty in all its forms. And in case you haven't noticed, Lauren Wadsworth is a knockout."

Of course I had noticed. Everyone knew Lauren had it all. From the very first time I met her when she was throwing her thirteenth birthday party at the club, I knew it. She was beautiful. She looked great in clothes (which she has plenty of). She was completely comfortable being the center of attention. And she was really nice to me.

I thought I felt something else in the envelope. I reached in and pulled out an RSVP card, which came with its own mini envelope. It was navy blue, too, but the best thing was that the stamp didn't have George Washington or Thomas Jefferson or some other dead president on it. It had a picture of Ben Feldman. Yes, I said that. On the stamp! Wow, those Feldmans had thought of everything.

"I am mailing off my RSVP first thing tomorrow," I said, tucking the card safely back in the envelope.

"So, I assume you're going?" Ryan said.

"Are you kidding? I am so going."

"Hope you don't have a tennis match that weekend. You know Dad has a fit if you go out on tournament weekends."

True, our dad is a bear about our training. Sammie and I are California-ranked tennis players in the Under-14 Girls Doubles category, and he's our coach. But even a hardhead like him would understand that there was no way we could miss the party of the year.

"What did Sammie think of the invitation?" I asked Ryan.

"Don't know. I only saw yours and mine on the kitchen table."

"She's taking GoGo for a walk. I'll bet she took it with her. That rat, I can't believe she left without telling me about it."

"Can't blame her," Ryan said. "A certain Miss Serious Student said no one should disturb her while she's studying for her Big Old Scary History Test."

By the way, GoGo is our grandma, our mom's mom. She doesn't usually live with us, but last month she was in a car accident and broke her leg, so she's staying with us while she's recovering. Sammie and I take turns every afternoon taking her for a walk along the boardwalk in her wheelchair so she can watch the sunset over the ocean. We don't mind doing it since she's the best and most fun grandma ever.

Besides, she tells us funny stories about when she pushed us up and down that same boardwalk when we were cute little tots in our stroller. Like once, a producer asked her if we could be in a TV commercial for bubble gum because they were looking for twins who were completely identical. GoGo said no, because she doesn't think sugary gum is good for kids' teeth. Another time, she stopped to buy a bag of french fries from Jody's Burger Stand, and while she was paying, she gave us each a fry to suck on. Sammie liked it so much, she gummed down almost the whole bag before GoGo had even gotten her change. Sammie hates it when we tell that story because she's sensitive about her weight. I'm not, but then I don't weigh as much as she does. I feel bad for her because our dad watches her weight like a hawk and comments on everything she eats. That can't be fun.

I grabbed my pink sweatshirt off the back of my chair and threw it on. I couldn't wait to see Sammie's reaction to Ben's invitation. She's been hanging around with a group of kids at school, kind of a weird bunch as far as I'm concerned, and I've been trying to get her to spend more time with me and the SF2s. I was sure that this amazing invitation would support my case that the SF2s were the group we wanted to be in.

"Tell Dad I'm going to find Sammie and GoGo," I hollered to Ryan as I left my room. He didn't look up, though. He had found a bag full of pretzel sticks that I brought in for a snack the night before and was shoving them in his mouth five at a time.

The screen door slammed behind me as I ran out of the house and headed for the beach. I had put the invitation carefully under my T-shirt. I didn't stuff it in the pocket of my sweatshirt like I usually would have. It was too beautiful, and I didn't want it to get as much as a wrinkle. It was going into my scrapbook so I could look at it forever.

I ran past the tennis courts where Dad was giving a lesson to Mrs. Addison, the mom of one of my other new friends, Brooke. Mrs. Addison and Brooke have two things in common—thick, blond hair and a tan the color of a latte. All of us are dying to have a tan like Brooke's, even though Sammie thinks it's a spray on. Brooke says it absolutely isn't, and I believe her.

"Hi, Dad!" I called out. "Nice backhand, Mrs. Addison." Okay, truthfully, her backhand was hopeless, but I like to be encouraging, especially to the mom of a new friend. Well, a new almost-friend.

Once I hit the boardwalk, which is nothing more

than a little wooden-planked path that leads down the beach to the Santa Monica pier, I broke into a run. I could see Sammie and GoGo stopped a little ways up, looking out between two palm trees to the ocean beyond.

"Hey, you two," I called out as I reached them. "I can't wait to show you the coolest thing."

"*Shhh*, Charlie," GoGo said, putting her finger up to her lips. She was wearing one of the silver rings she makes, this one with a gray moonstone that glowed pink in the sun's reflection. "Whatever you have can wait, darling child. We're observing the golden moment."

She turned back to the ocean, and I followed her gaze. The sky was doing that amazing thing the Southern California sky does at sunset. The ocean had turned steel gray, and the sky above it was a swirl of pink and orange and lavender, like different pots of paint had spilled and all the most brilliant colors had run into one another. In the distance, I could see the dark-purple outline of Catalina Island, where GoGo had taken us last year to see a herd of wild bison that roam there.

I couldn't get Sammie's attention as she stood there silently, so together we all waited and watched the sun flatten out and slide into the ocean. As soon as it disappeared, the temperature seemed to drop, and I shivered as I zipped up my sweatshirt and put the hood up. I could feel the blue envelope next to my body.

"Now can I show you guys what I have?" I asked impatiently.

"This better be good, after all the buildup," Sammie said. "I hope it's not one of your boring cheerleading routines."

Sammie has been on my case ever since Lauren and I decided to try out for the cheer squad. I was getting pretty tired of her comments.

"Cheerleading is not boring," I said. "However, I'm going to overlook your negative attitude because I am in such a great mood. No, make that supergreat. No, fantastically stupendously supergreat."

"My, my," said GoGo. "Let us in on the secret that has put you into this blissful state of mind."

I flashed Sammie a knowing smile. "I think Sammie knows what I'm so excited about, don't you?"

Sammie just shrugged her shoulders. "No clue," she answered.

Okay, I could play this game, too.

"It's blue and gold and pops out at you." I giggled.

"Um . . . a Halloween ghost in a Dodger jacket," Sammie said.

"No, but close. Guess again."

"Charlie, honey, it's getting cold out here," GoGo said. "Can you just tell us what it is?"

I reached under my sweatshirt, pulled out the invitation, and handed it to GoGo. Sammie looked at it over her shoulder. I couldn't believe that she seemed so . . . I don't know . . . unexcited.

"Weren't you totally blown away when you saw it?" I asked her.

"I'm just seeing it now for the first time. I haven't even finished reading it yet."

"But you must have read yours. Don't tell me you didn't even open it yet?"

"I didn't get one, Charlie."

"Of course you did. It's probably in the kitchen somewhere. Ben wouldn't have invited me without inviting you."

I noticed a weird expression come over GoGo's face, like she was worried or something. She took Sammie's hand and gave it a squeeze.

"Well, there certainly is no reason Sammie wouldn't be invited," she said in a firm voice. "She is such wonderful company, I'm sure every student at Beachside would want her at their party."

I nodded. Sammie was kind of squirming, like she was in a hurry to change the subject. I felt bad for her, and I wanted to fix the situation right away.

"I'll meet you guys back at the house," I said. "I'm going to go check this out, Sammie. I'm sure your invitation just got misplaced somewhere."

Sammie didn't answer, but I noticed she was doing that lip-biting thing she does when she gets nervous. I do the same thing. Last week during my pre-algebra unit test, I almost chewed my entire bottom lip off.

As I jogged back to the house, I reviewed the possibilities. Sammie's invitation was probably under a pile of mail or lodged in between the sports section and the business section of the newspaper. If it wasn't there, then maybe it got delayed and would arrive the next day. Stuff like that happens all the time. Things get put into the wrong bin at the post office. They'd have to make mistakes, with all those millions of letters floating around inside.

As I got to the door of our cottage, Dad was walking Mrs. Addison to her car. I waved and dashed inside to take a frantic look around.

Our whole place is tiny—there's the bedroom I share with Sammie, our mom and dad's bedroom, which used to be an old locker room, the living room where Ryan usually sleeps on the foldout couch, and a kitchen with a breakfast nook.

It didn't take me long to inspect the kitchen counter, check under the couch pillows, and search around the blow-up bed where Ryan was camping out while GoGo stayed with us. He is such a pig; he tossed his blankets all over the floor and didn't bother to fold them up until Dad yelled at him to do it. I even went out to the mailbox and reached my hand deep inside the dolphin-shaped box to see if Sammie's invitation had gotten stuck in the back behind the advertising flyers and pizza delivery ads.

Nothing.

Outside, I could see Sammie pushing GoGo's wheelchair up onto our deck. Quickly, I ran into my room and called Lauren. She would know what was happening. Lauren Wadsworth knew everything that went on at Beachside.

I barely gave her time to say hello.

"Lauren," I said. "I have a quick question for you."

"Hi, Charlie," she said. "I was hoping it was you. I bet I know what your question is. It's about what we're going to wear to Ben's bar mitzvah, right?"

"You're half right. It is about Ben's bar mitzvah. But I was wondering if . . ." Suddenly, I felt awkward bringing it up, but then I thought of Sammie and got the courage to go on. "If . . . um . . . if you knew what happened to Sammie's invitation. She didn't get it."

There was a long silence on the other end of the phone, so I went on.

"It's really embarrassing that I got mine and she didn't get hers," I babbled, "so I was just checking to make sure everything's okay . . . with her invitation, I mean."

"Charlie," Lauren said, "I'm just going to tell you this straight out because you're my friend. Sammie didn't get an invitation because she's not invited."

I almost dropped the phone. How could they? How could they leave her out and invite me?

"That's not f-fair," I stammered.

"Think about it, Charlie. It's Ben's party. He's allowed to invite who he wants."

"But this is going to hurt her feelings," I said. I sounded like I was begging.

"Sammie has her own friends," Lauren said. "And face it, Charlie, she doesn't fit in with us like you do. I don't mean to sound cold about it, but even you have to admit that's the truth."

I had no answer for that. She was right. Sammie was hanging around with Alicia Bermudez and a bunch of kids in Ms. Carew's Truth Tellers group, an after-school club where they work on expressing their true feelings and dig into their "issues." They are pretty alternative and, well . . . I don't want to say dorky because that's not nice . . . but I think you get the picture.

"Sammie's my sister," I said to Lauren. "My friends are her friends. It's always been like that with us."

"That's very noble, Charlie, but listen to this. Spencer called me to make sure you're going. I think he likes you. You two would make such a cute couple."

Okay, I confess. For a second I forgot all about Sammie. I've had my eye on Spencer Ballard since the first time I saw him. He has this curly, blond hair and a dimple when he smiles and great abs, which I only know about because he displays them when he plays Frisbee on the beach. Even Sammie, who has terrible taste in boys, said she thinks he's the cutest of all the SF2s.

I held the phone silently, feeling ashamed that the news about Spencer had distracted me from my mission.

"Listen, Charlie, I've got to go," Lauren said. "My dad is making me set the table, can you believe it? He's totally into this get-good-grades-and-do-your-chores kick. I'll call you later and we'll talk."

As I put down the phone, I could hear Sammie talking to GoGo in the living room, helping her out of the wheelchair and onto the couch. Soon, we'd all be having dinner together, chatting about our days. What would I tell Sammie? That she was left out of the best party of the year? That my new friends were rejecting her?

I picked up the beautiful blue envelope with its shimmering gold letters and just stood there staring at it. And you know what? Suddenly, it didn't look so beautiful anymore.

The Worst
Dinner Ever

....

Chapter 2

"I have an idea," my dad announced as we settled into our places at the dinner table. Actually, it isn't much of a dinner table, more of a breakfast nook built for four that the five of us were crammed into.

"How about if everybody reports one good thing that happened today," he said as we all let out huge groans. "I'll start."

That's typical of our dad. He is a big fan of his own ideas.

"The best thing about my day is this delicious-looking *albóndigas* soup that Esperanza made for dinner," he began, passing us each an empty bowl. "Espie, you're a lifesaver for staying late to help us out while GoGo is laid up."

Esperanza, who is the cleaning person at the

Sporty Forty, rolled her eyes as she put out some homemade *pupusas* to go with the soup. She thinks it's odd that my dad calls her Espie, because no one else in the world does. He gives nicknames to everyone, though, whether they like it or not. It's a jock thing. Ryan is Ry Guy, and he calls our mom Cinnamon Bun when he's in a good mood and Boss when they're fighting.

"Mr. Diamond, can I call Candido to pick me up soon?" Esperanza asked as she dished out bowls of steaming meatball soup. "I do the dishes when I come back tomorrow."

"No problem, Espie. The kids will clean up. There's only one person with a broken leg here. Everyone else does their share. Right, guys?"

We all groaned again, and Esperanza laughed as she headed onto the deck to make her call.

"Tell Candido to bring Alicia," Sammie called after her.

"Good idea," Ryan chimed in. "She doesn't have a broken leg, so that means she can help with the dishes."

Alicia Bermudez is Esperanza and Candido's daughter. Candido is the groundskeeper at the Sporty Forty and Esperanza works there three days a week. Alicia is in the seventh grade like us and gets to go to Beachside because her parents work in the district. Personally, I think she and Sammie are hanging out way too much these days, which is kind of uncomfortable for me. Don't get me wrong . . . I really like Alicia, but as I mentioned before, she and her drama-kid friends are . . . well . . . let's just say *different* and leave it at that.

"Okay, team, who else has something good to report?" Dad went on. He seemed to be enjoying his own little game.

Before I could stop him, Ryan shot off his big mouth. "Charlie had something great happen today. Isn't that right, Charles? The invitation of the century."

I gave Ryan a nasty look that told him in no uncertain terms I didn't want to talk about it. But he's so thick, he didn't get it. He just sailed right along with his mouth flapping in the sea breeze.

"Yup, I'm proud of my little sis here. Barely a month at a new school and, just like me, she's already in the thick of it. The party girl in the swirl."

"That makes no sense, Ryan," I snapped.

"I know, but it rhymed, so that's cool. Maybe I should become a rapper."

"Or not."

I noticed that Sammie had put down her spoon and was looking in her soup bowl, staring down a meatball.

"So who's having the big party?" Dad asked.

"It's just Ben Feldman's bar mitzvah," I muttered. "No big deal."

"Whoa, like a party at Dodger Stadium is no big deal?" Ryan exclaimed, for some weird reason making his voice suddenly sound like Kermit the Frog. "An hour ago you were over the moon about it."

"Well, I've changed my mind," I said. "I'm not going."

What? Did those words just come out of my mouth? Yes, I believe they did. Good-bye, Dodger Stadium. Good-bye, private locker room tour. Good-bye, amusements galore. Good-bye, cute Spencer.

Sammie looked at me with a combination of surprise and annoyance.

"You can go, Charlie," she said. "You don't have to miss it because of me." Her voice had that bite in it that it gets when she's irritated.

"It sounds like quite a shindig," my dad said. "You both should go."

That was followed by an uncomfortable silence. Can someone tell me why it is that when it comes to social things, dads never seem to get the picture? Is there a male gene for being clueless?

"Good thought, Dad." Ryan was still talking in his Kermit voice, which by the way, is really bad. "But it seems only one of them has been invited. Besides me, that is."

"You don't know that," I said quickly. "Maybe Sammie's invitation got lost in the mail." I knew that wasn't what happened, but it just seemed so cruel to say the truth.

"Can we not talk about this anymore?" Sammie said. "I think we should change the subject."

"You've got nothing to be ashamed of, Sam-I-am," Ryan said, giving her a playful punch in the arm. "Even though I'm invited, I'm not sure I'm going to go. Being an eighth-grader, I'm not sure how it'll look going to a seventh-grade party."

Sammie really tensed up at that, and you couldn't blame her. It's bad enough not to get invited to a party, but it's even worse to have the whole family discussing it over dinner. I think Ryan was actually trying to make her feel better about it.

"But I still think it blows," he went on. "Ben Feldman should either have asked both of you or neither of you. Maybe you're not as slick as Charles here, but you're cool in your own kind of way."

Suddenly, Sammie stood up, almost knocking over her soup bowl. "If it's okay with everyone here, I'd rather not have my entire social life, or lack of a social life, be the topic of our dinner conversation." Her face was turning beet red, which happens to both of us when we get mad.

"Listen, Sammie," I said. "Right after dinner I'm going to call Lauren, and she'll talk to Ben. We'll fix this."

"I don't need Lauren Wadsworth to fix anything for me, Charlie. And I don't need your pity, either. I don't care whether I go or not. It's just a party. It's no big deal!"

She was yelling now, and I could see her chin start to tremble, like she was going to cry. But instead, she crumpled up her napkin, tossed it down on her seat, and stomped off.

"Sammie, you hardly ate any dinner," GoGo called after her. "Come back and sit down. Let's talk this through like adults."

Sammie didn't even answer. She just marched across the living room to our bedroom, went in, and slammed the door.

We were all quiet until Ryan spoke. "Does this mean she doesn't have to do the dishes?" he asked in a weak attempt at humor.

I felt terrible. A lot of people say that identical twins have special feelings for each other. I don't know if that's true, but at that very moment, I felt all the rejection and embarrassment that I was sure Sammie was experiencing. I got up from the table and ran after her. Ordinarily, GoGo would have come, too, because she always has a lot of wisdom in these matters, but she was stuck in her wheelchair and not very mobile. As I bolted to our room, I heard my dad say to Ryan, "Everything is so emotional with those two."

I found Sammie flopped facedown on her bed, holding her history book. She didn't look up when I came in.

"Can we talk about this?" I asked.

"I'm studying."

"No, you're not."

"Yes, I am. My history midterm is Monday and even Mr. Mintner says it's really hard. We have to know all the pharaohs of ancient Egypt in order."

"Well, then maybe if you're studying so hard, you should turn your book right side up," I commented.

It wasn't true that her book was upside down, but the fact that she had to check it told me that she hadn't even looked at it. She was thinking about the kings of Egypt like I was thinking about the rings of Saturn.

"Look, Sammie," I said. "I feel awful about this, and I want you to know that I don't have to go to Ben's party."

"If you don't go, what will you tell Lauren and all your other new friends in the SF2s?"

"The truth. That I don't think it's right he didn't invite you, too."

"Oh, that's just great, Charlie. Nothing embarrassing about that. I enjoy being seen as the dork outsider who doesn't fit in and is a complete social obstacle to her prettier sister."

"That's not fair, Sammie, and you know it."

She picked up her history book and stuck her nose in it, but I could tell she wasn't reading. Her eyes weren't even moving. I paced back and forth in our room, which is so small that you can cross it in exactly three and a half steps. I considered my options. Either way, I was stuck. If I went to Ben's party, I'd feel like a traitor to Sammie. If I didn't go, I'd be making Sammie the object of everyone's attention. The last thing she wanted was to feel pathetic.

There was a knock on the door. It was probably Ryan who had come to *not* amuse us with more of his bad Kermit imitation.

"Go away," we both shouted in unison.

"Sammie, it's me, Alicia," came the voice from the other side of the door.

Sammie sprang to her feet and practically flew to the door.

"I'm so glad to see you," she said, throwing her arms around Alicia. "I am having a totally miserable night."

"I know," Alicia said. "My mom told me what's going on." Then she looked at me a little nervously. "It's not like she was trying to eavesdrop or anything. She just couldn't help overhearing the conversation."

"It's fine, Alicia," I told her. Alicia sat down on Sammie's bed. Her dark hair was pulled back in a ponytail, and she was wearing gray sweats, a splattered white T-shirt, and running shoes. There wasn't a stitch of makeup on her face, and she didn't even have her usual gold earrings in her pierced ears. Personally, I wouldn't visit a friend looking like that, but it didn't seem to bother her. I think she noticed that I was checking her out, because she looked down at the red splotch on her T-shirt, then up at me.

"I know," she said, laughing. "It's gross. This is what happens when I cook dinner. You can see every ingredient on my T-shirt. See, there's the tomato sauce. But, hey, the spaghetti was good."

We all laughed, even Sammie, which was good because it lightened the mood.

"So, Charlie," Alicia said. "Let's talk about this. Sammie and I are Truth Tellers."

"I know all about it. You guys sit around in Ms. Carew's room after school and pour your hearts out to one another. No offense, but I'd rather go to cheerleading practice."

"No offense taken," Alicia said. "We appreciate the truth . . . which means that we have to tell the truth here, too. So tell us honestly, do you want to go to Ben's party?"

"I already told Sammie I wouldn't go," I answered.

"But you want to go, right? Tell the truth."

I looked over at Sammie to see if she was hating this conversation. She was. I didn't blame her. It feels terrible to be excluded. I could tell she was jealous and hurt by the way she was frowning and squirming at the same time.

"Alicia, could we not talk about this anymore?" she asked.

"Ms. Carew always says that the truths that are hardest to express are the ones that make you feel uncomfortable," Alicia said. "That's why it's so important to get them out."

"Okay, the truth," Sammie said, taking a deep breath. "I don't really know Ben Feldman, and one part of me doesn't care about his party. But the other part of me feels left out. That feels just plain bad."

"How about you, Charlie?" Alicia said. "What's your truth?"

"I feel bad for Sammie," I said. "I really and truly do."

"But you want to go to the party?"

"Well, it does sound kind of fun," I said timidly.

"The truth, Charlie," Alicia insisted.

"Okay," I said. "Here's the truth: The truth is that Ben's party sounds totally awesome."

Sammie nodded. "It does," she agreed. "That's why I don't want you to sacrifice going because of me. That would make me feel really lousy."

We both just sat there silently for a minute until Alicia spoke up.

"This is good," she said. "You both said how you really feel."

I didn't see what was so great about it. We still didn't have a solution, we both just felt bad.

"I have a great idea," Alicia said. "Sammie doesn't have to miss out on a fabulous party or feel left out. Charlie, I think you should go to Ben's party and have a great time. We'll throw our own party and have a great time ourselves. A we're-not-invited-but-we-don't-care party."

"Just you and me?" Sammie asked Alicia.

Understandably, she didn't sound all that enthusiastic.

"No, we'll get all the kids in Truth Tellers together, and we'll do something really fun. Like a costume party. Do you think your dad would let us have it here? We could make a bonfire on the beach and—"

"Roast hot dogs and make s'mores," Sammie interrupted, her eyes lighting up. There's nothing my sister likes more than gooey foods like mac and cheese or Rice Krispies Treats, but s'mores are her all-time favorite.

"Yeah, who needs Ben Feldman to have a good time?" Alicia said, holding up her hand for a high five.

"Right," Sammie agreed, high-fiving her. "We can have our own fun."

"So, Charlie," Alicia said. "You go to Dodger Stadium and have amusements galore. We'll have our own right here."

"You sure this is okay with you?" I asked Sammie.

"I'm going to give it my best shot," she said. And then she smiled. I couldn't tell if it was a totally real smile or the kind you put on when you're trying to smile.

"So then I'm going to tell Ben I'm going?" I asked.

"I believe that's the usual procedure," she said with her typical wisecracking tone. It was the old Sammie, the fun one.

A huge feeling of relief swept over me. Immediately, Sammie and Alicia started talking about themes for the party, and I ran into the living room to get my phone. I couldn't wait to tell Lauren that I could go. Lauren and I were going to have so much fun deciding what to wear and how to do our hair and who we were going to sit next to on the bus. (Oh, did I mention that the invitation said a luxury party bus was going to take everyone to Dodger Stadium?) Of course, I wanted to sit next to Lauren, but then there was also the possibility that Spencer Ballard would fight her for the chance to sit next to me. That was too much to hope for.

When I called Lauren, it took her a few rings to answer. As soon as she picked up, I could tell something was wrong. Her nose was all stuffy, and she sounded like she had been crying.

"Lauren, what is it?"

"I have horrible news, Charlie."

"What happened?"

"It's my stupid dad. He's all mad about my grades and says I have to get at least straight Bs or I'm in big trouble."

"Okay, we can deal with that," I told her. "I'll help you study, and eventually your grades will get better."

"Yeah, but he wants them better on *this* report card. There's no way I'm going to get a B in history. Not with that impossible midterm coming up. If I don't get a B, then I can't . . ."

And then she burst into tears, sobbing so loud I couldn't understand the end of the sentence.

"What, Lauren? What can't you do?"

"I can't go to Ben's bar mitzvah."

"He wouldn't do that to you."

"He would and he did."

I was silent. I didn't know what to say. I knew how awful I had felt when I thought about missing Ben's party. But for Lauren to miss it, Lauren who was the leader of the SF2s ... well, it was just unthinkable.

"We'll come up with some way out of this," I said, even though I didn't see any way out. Lauren is not a good student in general, and she had been goofing off pretty seriously in history. She was going to have to ace that midterm, and acing midterms isn't exactly what Lauren does best.

I heard her dad calling her in the background. I couldn't make out every word, but he sounded pretty irritated.

"Listen, Charlie. I have to go." She sniffled. "We'll talk tomorrow. Meet me before school at our table."

Then she hung up. Slowly, I walked back into my room. Alicia and Sammie were busy talking excitedly about their party. They were even going to make a banner that said WE'RE NOT INVITED BUT WE DON'T CARE. I picked up Ben's invitation from my dresser, and as I ran my fingers over the beautiful paper, I wondered how it was possible that one envelope could be filled with so much trouble.

Sticking Together

....

Chapter 3

"What are you doing up so early?" Sammie asked, rolling over in bed and rubbing her eyes sleepily. My sister is definitely not a morning person.

"I'm meeting Lauren before school. She's in a crisis."

"What happened? She chip her nail polish?"

"Funny. Remind me to say something nasty about your friends next time."

Sammie yawned and threw the pillow over her head. She had gone to bed late the night before. After Alicia went home, Sammie sat down at our computer and got into designing an invitation to their "Not Invited" party. She had decided that the front should say COME TO OUR COSTUME EXTRAVAGANZA, but she was having trouble because the word *extravaganza* was too long to fit on her screen, and besides, she wasn't sure if everyone would know what it meant.

Sammie had already fallen back asleep in the time it took me to grab my backpack, brush my hair, and open the door to our room. As I tiptoed into the living room, I was hoping our dad was still asleep, but there he was, sitting on the couch, eating a bowl of granola.

"Hi, Dad. Bye, Dad. I have to be at school early."

"Got your tennis clothes?" he asked.

"Don't need them."

"Isn't today the day you girls are working out with the tennis team?"

"It's tomorrow, Dad. Friday, remember? And we're not working out. We're participating with the girls' tennis team in an exhibition match at Lincoln Middle School."

"Oh, right," he said, going back to his granola. He is totally focused on our tennis in real tournaments because he wants us to do well and get college scholarships. But as far as exhibition matches at school or just regular fun tennis, his only interest is that we don't get injured.

"You'll have to be careful not to get injured," he called after me as I left.

What did I tell you?

I walked the four blocks to school really fast. There was a thick morning fog, typical for late October at the beach, and I didn't want my hair to get all frizzy from the dampness. Plus, I wanted to get there early because I was worried about Lauren. She had already texted me that she had gone to her dad and begged him to change his mind, but he had refused. She said she had been crying all night.

When I got to school, I hurried to the outside lunch pavilion next to the cafeteria. It's where everyone eats except when it's raining. The SF2s sit at the same table every day, and I've been sitting with them almost every lunch. I still can't believe it's my table. It feels awesome to be included.

I was surprised to see the other girls from the club already there with Lauren. Jillian Kendall was sitting next to her, drinking her usual morning strawberry-banana smoothie. Not that I'm jealous, but I just want to say that Jillian spends more on smoothies in a month than I spend on my entire wardrobe for the semester. Brooke was sitting across the table from Jillian, looking into her cell phone and putting on gold lip gloss. She has this cool app that turns your iPhone screen into a mirror, and because she's obsessed with lip gloss, she gets a lot of use out of it. She uses it way more than the calculator app, that's for sure. At the end of the table was Lily March, who always dresses so creatively, but today looked especially great in her silver ballet flats and rolled-up jeans. She was flipping through a three-ring notebook and writing down a list of numbers on a yellow pad, twirling one finger around and around her curly black hair. She was concentrating so hard she didn't even look up.

I don't know why I was hurt to see everyone else there before me. I guess I thought that Lauren had called only me, and that the *two* of us were going to work out her problem together. I hadn't realized everyone else would be invited. But then, Lauren had been best friends with these girls ever since elementary school, and of course she was going to call them in a time of crisis. I told myself that I shouldn't feel hurt.

"Have you heard?" Brooke said as I slid onto the bench next to her. "Lauren's father has gone totally mental. Do you think my lips are too sparkly?"

"The gold looks good with your tan," I told her. Brooke looks like all the pictures of California girls that are always featured in fashion magazines and on TV. Blond hair, white teeth, golden tan, sparkly lips. I've never met anyone who glows like she does.

Lauren was dabbing her eyes with a tissue. She didn't look good. Well, she didn't look good *for Lauren*. She's so pretty that it's hard for her to ever look really bad. Her eyes were red rimmed and puffy, and she had bitten her nails down to little nubs.

"Oh, Charlie, this is a total disaster," she said when she saw me, her eyes welling with tears. "I tried to tell him that I'm terrible at history, but he wouldn't even listen. He said I was lazy and only interested in my social life."

"What are you supposed to be interested in?" Brooke said. "A bunch of old Egyptian dudes with weird names like Ramses and Tutan-blah-blah, who wore headdresses and locked themselves up in pyramids with their servants and their jewels?"

"It's Tutankhamen, airhead," Jillian said, polishing off the last of her smoothie. "They called him the 'boy king.' Remember, he had this completely gorgeous burial mask that was made of real gold."

"Look who's the expert on ancient Egypt." Brooke snorted.

"I got really interested in their jewelry," Jillian explained. "Man, those Egyptians had some serious bling."

Actually, I was impressed that Jillian knew anything about the pharaohs of ancient Egypt. Of all the kids in the SF2s, she's by far the worst student, probably because she spends every night watching reality shows about housewives and models and teen moms. Right after I met her, she told me she was allergic to homework, which is a funny thing to say except at report-card time, when I imagine that joke doesn't give her mom and dad a real big laugh.

"What am I going to do, you guys?" Lauren said. "My future is bleak."

I didn't have a good answer, so I just reached out

and gave Lauren's hand a squeeze.

"Okay, here's the deal," Lily said, putting down her pencil and flipping the notebook closed. "I've written down your scores on all the quizzes and tests in your notebook. You got a B on one quiz, so it proves you can do it."

Lauren's eyes brightened a little.

"However," Lily went on, "you've also gotten two Cs, one F, and a C-minus on the unit test on the beginnings of civilization."

"That test was really hard," I said, trying to make Lauren feel better.

"And boring," Jillian added, tossing the empty plastic cup into the nearby trash. I wanted to take it out of the trash and put it in the recycling container next to it, but I didn't want anyone to think I liked fishing around in random trash cans.

"You have a C-minus average," Lily said to Lauren. "That's the bad news. The good news is that if you get an A on the test Monday, you'll get a B-minus in the class."

"Which technically counts as a B," Jillian said.

"Dodger Stadium here you come," Brooke said, giving Lauren a hug. "Problem solved. Nice work, Lilykins."

"There's one thing, guys," Lauren said, still sounding a little unsure. "How do I get an A on the test? I'm not good at history."

"You'll just have to study really hard," I told her.

"If you memorize everything, you'll do okay."

"Will you study with me, Charlie? You're really smart."

"Sammie and I have a tournament all day Sunday at Sand and Surf Tennis Club," I said. "And we have to train on Saturday. But it's only Thursday today, so we have after school today and tomorrow to study. I'll come over."

"Oh, I can't tomorrow night," Lauren said. "I'm supposed to meet Ryan at the football game. He's invited me to sit with the eighth-grade boys. I can't miss that."

"But, Lauren, this is really important," I urged.

"Like the football game isn't? Come on, Charlie. It's a big step in my social life."

The lunch pavilion was starting to fill up with students arriving for school. The cafeteria sells these really great cinnamon buns and a lot of kids come early to buy them for breakfast. I noticed that Brooke had lost interest in our conversation and was standing up, waving to a group of boys walking in from the carpool line. One of them was the General, her sort-of boyfriend. His real name is Dwayne Dickerson, but all the SF2s call him the General because he always dresses in camouflage cargo pants. He was walking next to another guy, Sean Patterson, who is the best athlete in the whole school. He's the top scorer in three sports—soccer, basketball, and baseball. I'm an athlete, too, so I can tell you that's pretty hard to do.

You have to have a real natural talent.

"What's up with the sad faces?" Sean said as he and the General arrived at our table. "Looks like somebody died. Or lost a game."

"Lauren's having parent problems," Brooke answered, looking directly at the General even though it was Sean who asked the question. "She has to bring up her grades."

"I feel your pain," the General said. "My dad's on the same campaign. You can do it, though, Laur. It's all about time management."

"That's what I was telling her," I chimed in. "If she skips the football game tomorrow and doesn't make any other plans, she can just do nothing but study her head off."

"Whoa, easy there, chief," the General said. "That's pretty extreme. We don't want her brain to explode."

Everyone laughed, and within five seconds, the topic switched to where they were all going to meet up before the game. I was frustrated because I knew how hard I'd already been studying for that history test, and Lauren hadn't even opened a book. Our teacher had even said that spelling counts, and if you've ever tried to spell the names of the pharaohs of ancient Egypt, you know how hard that is. There are all kinds of *h*'s and *k*'s and *m*'s that you can't even begin to sound out.

When Ben Feldman arrived at the table, wearing his usual plaid shorts even though it was a damp, foggy morning, everyone stood up and applauded. Sean did a fake bow as if Ben were the king of a major country.

"All hail to the chief of party givers," he said.

Everyone complimented him on the awesome invitation. It turns out that Ben's dad works for the Dodger front office (I'm not sure what that is, but I was too embarrassed to ask), and that's why he got to hold the party at Dodger Stadium. It was cool because Ben seemed really excited about the event. When he said he was studying hard for his bar mitzvah and had to memorize a lot of passages in Hebrew, I whispered to Lauren, "See, you're not the only one who has to study hard." But she didn't pay any attention because she was distracted by Ryan's arrival in the lunch pavilion.

He strutted in like he owned the school, his sunglasses draped around the back of his neck. Sammie was tagging along behind him. Honestly, she looked like she had just rolled out of bed, which I'm sure she had. If you ask me, she could have at least pulled her hair back into a ponytail instead of letting it just sit there on her head looking like a squirrel had built a nest in it.

"Hey, rich kids," Ryan called out as he approached our table. "How's life in the fast lane?"

I was the only one who cringed at that remark. Everyone else laughed—and not *at* Ryan but *with* him. Ryan has an amazing ability to make people love him. Even though Sammie and I think he's a total goofball at home, the kids at school think he's so funny. He's just got that Ryan touch that makes you feel like you've known him forever. He doesn't care what he says, because whatever comes out of his mouth sounds friendly and totally natural.

Sammie found Alicia right away, standing with another one of their friends, Sara Berlin. She's a tall girl who has hair so big and frizzy that she looks like one of those poofy French poodles at a dog show. I saw Sammie immediately pull a paper out of her backpack and launch into an animated conversation with them. No doubt she was showing them her designs for the party invitation and trying to figure out a way to fit *EXTRAVAGANZA* on the page. I was grateful she wasn't passing it around at my table.

When the bell rang and it was time to head for homeroom, I naturally took my place next to Lauren. Spencer came up and walked in between us for a bit, and I could feel my cheeks getting all pink. He had no idea how completely adorable he was, just laughing about how his dog had chased a cat up a tree and then got scared when the cat hissed at him. It's really nice to see a guy who loves animals the way Spencer loves his dog. On a shallower note, it's also nice to see his dimple come out when he laughs.

I wanted our conversation to go on forever, but Spencer is in Mr. Boring's homeroom with Lauren, and that's in the bungalows, so he and Lauren and a couple of the others had to head off in another direction. I'm in Ms. Hamel's homeroom, which is in the main building, and to my complete surprise, I found myself walking into the building with Sean. He seemed to kind of push Brooke and the General aside so he could get to me. I checked my hair nervously as we walked and hoped my lip gloss was still shiny.

"Too bad about Lauren," he said, falling into perfect step with me.

"She's going to have to really apply herself."

Oh my goodness, Charlie. Did you say that? I don't know how that sentence managed to come out of my mouth. It sounded like my dad talking. He always tells Sammie and me that we are going to have to *apply* ourselves if we want to move up in the rankings. Sean didn't seem to mind, though.

"My older brother, Clark, had a grade issue for a while," he went on. "He got kicked off the football team."

"Are your parents strict?"

"No, it wasn't my parents. It was the school. They wouldn't let him play unless he maintained a C average. He almost missed the whole season."

"What'd he do?"

"He brought his grades up. Easy peasy."

"That's good. I'll bet he studied really hard."

"Not really. He got a little help."

"You mean, like a tutor?"

Sean laughed. "That would be the hard way, Charlie. I already told you it was easy peasy."

I didn't understand what he was talking about, but I didn't want to look like a total idiot. We were almost at homeroom, which is in Room Thirteen, at the end of the hall in the main building. As we passed by an open door, Sean nodded at it with his head.

"In there," he said. "That's what saved Clark."

"That's just the teachers' lounge," I said. "Nothing happens in there except at lunch when the teachers eat salads out of plastic containers."

"That's where you're wrong." Sean smiled. "That room also happens to contain the humongous printer. The really fast one that spits out, like, two hundred pages a minute."

"And why would I care about that?"

"Check it out, Charlie. It's the place where the teachers print out their tests. And I happen to know that once they're printed, they keep them in file cabinets in the closet."

"Good for them," I said. "That sounds like a great system."

"What I'm saying," Sean said cautiously, looking me

square in the eye, "is that if someone were motivated, they could easily sneak in there when the teachers are all in class and no one is inside and get a copy of a test."

Sean locked his eyes onto mine as if we were sharing a big secret.

"Is that what your brother did?" I asked.

"No way."

Wow, I was relieved to hear that. Stealing a copy of a test was big-time cheating, and I was glad to know Sean's brother hadn't done that.

"His friends did it for him," Sean whispered as we headed into homeroom.

"They stole a test for him?" I couldn't believe what I was hearing.

"They *borrowed* it, Charlie. And don't look so shocked. He learned the material by himself; he just had a little help beforehand."

We were already inside Ms. Hamel's class when Sean put his hand on my shoulder and gave it a squeeze.

"Lauren could use a little help," he whispered. "If you're really her friend, you'd help her."

"You mean steal a test?" I whispered.

"Borrow," he answered. "The word is *borrow.*"

The bell rang as I staggered over to my desk and tried to make my face look normal. I couldn't believe what had just happened. Ms. Hamel launched into a long explanation about parent permission slips for the upcoming field trip to the art museum, but I didn't hear a word she said. There was only one word that spun around and around in my head.

Borrow.

Peer Pressure

....

Chapter 4

"Hey, Charlie," the General called as I headed to my locker before lunch. "Wait up. I'll walk with you."

He slammed his locker shut, slung his camouflage backpack over his shoulder, and hurried over to me. Everyone was racing by to get to the cafeteria first. Thursday is taco day, and you want to get there before they run out of the shredded chicken. Ryan always says that what they call shredded beef is really yak meat, which is his charming way of saying that it doesn't taste like any meat you can recognize. That's why everyone races for the chicken.

"So, you having an okay morning?" the General asked as we darted in between people and navigated over to my locker. I didn't answer, just concentrated on dialing the combination. I was still feeling uncomfortable about my conversation with Sean that morning, and it seemed strange that now the General was seeking me out. It wasn't like him to be so curious about how my morning was going, and I felt like something was up.

It didn't take me long to find out I was right. As I stuck my head inside my locker to fish out my gym clothes, he leaned in close.

"Sean tells me he talked to you," he began.

"That's not unusual. We're in homeroom together. And math, too."

"You know what I mean, Charliekins. About the teachers' lounge thing. We all need to pitch in to help Lauren out. You wouldn't want her to miss Ben's party because of you, would you?"

"Because of *me*?" I pulled my head out of my locker and just stared at him. "I didn't do anything to get her grounded."

"Of course you didn't. But you can do something to help. I mean, she's your best friend . . . or at least she will be when she realizes what you did to get her out of a bad situation."

"I don't steal, Dwayne." I thought using his real name would emphasize the point. But before he could answer, Brooke came out of the girls' bathroom and bolted over to us.

"So are you on board, Charlie?" she whispered. "We're all so grateful to you." What was going on? Were they all in on this?

"Do you guys know what you're asking me to do?" I asked. "It's not right. And it's dangerous, too. What if I get caught?"

"You won't," the General said. "We have it all planned. Tomorrow in history, sixth period, Brooke and Sean and I will ask Mr. Newhart a ton of questions about the test. You'll get a bathroom pass. All you have to do is tiptoe into the teachers' lounge, poke your nose in the door to make sure no one's there, and *presto*! You go in, you get it, you leave. You're quick and you're light on your feet. Just open up the file."

"Mr. Newhart's is the third drawer down," Brooke added. "I watched him this morning and saw him putting a stack of papers in there."

"Then you just reach in, pull out the unit test on Egypt, stick it under your shirt, and you're done," the General said, snapping his fingers. "Easy peasy."

"That seems to be the phrase of the day," I commented.

"You're totally safe," Brooke said. "We'll protect you."

"But it's cheating," I protested.

"You can call it that," the General answered. "You could also call it being a real friend who would do anything to help out another friend in trouble."

"Isn't that the kind of friend you want to be to us?" Brooke added. "One we know we can count on? One that shares everything, even our deepest, darkest secrets?"

"Does Lauren know about this?" I asked.

"We want to surprise her," Brooke said. "She's going to be so blown away, Charlie. She already loves you, but after this, you'll be a friend for life. Remember, this stays with us. You promise never to tell?"

I didn't answer.

"Charlie, you promise?" she repeated.

I nodded. I owed it to them to keep it a secret. They were my friends, and, right or wrong, I didn't want to get them in trouble. I slammed my locker closed as tears began to sting the corners of my eyes. I felt trapped.

"I have to think about this, guys," I said. "You go on, I'll meet you at the table."

Brooke gave me a hug.

"Remember, not a soul," she said. "Not even you-know-who coming down the hall."

She and the General left, and I turned around to see who she was referring to. It was Sammie, heading to lunch with Alicia and Sara and a kid named Will Lee, a very short sixth-grader. What was wrong with Sammie? I mean, if she wanted to hang out with Alicia and Sara, that was fine, her choice. But going to lunch with a sixth-grader who looked like he could be in the third grade? That was social suicide.

"What's wrong?" Sammie said the minute she saw me.

"Nothing. Why do you think something's wrong?"

"Um, because you're my twin. Because I've

been with you every day of my life. Because I know you as well as I know myself. Because I've seen that expression on your face before. Because when you're upset you frown and that freckle over your eyebrow squinches up and gets really close to your nose. Want me to go on?"

"I think it's so great how well you guys know each other," Sara said. "I wish I had a sister."

"I have a sister," Will piped up, "and she's a wicked pain in the neck. All she ever talks about is how good her grades are. If she gets an A instead of an A-plus, it's a flipping catastrophe." And then he did an impression of her wailing and moaning and clutching his heart. Alicia and Sara cracked up, and I had to admit, it was pretty funny.

"Hey," I said on a sudden impulse. "Is it okay if I eat with you guys today?"

Sammie looked surprised.

"What about your table?" she said. "Won't they look down on you slumming around with us nerds?"

"People need a shot of nerdiness every now and then," I joked. The truth was, I didn't want to sit at my table with all the SF2s. I didn't know who was in on the plan to steal the test and who wasn't. I didn't want to have to face any of them. It was just too much pressure.

Sammie's friends were no pressure at all. They were all so accepting, I could just sit there and be any old way I wanted to be. Of course, they were plenty strange, not the kind of kids I'd want to hang with every day. But I had a lot to think about, and I didn't need the pressure of wondering if I was being cool enough for my group. As we walked along the hall toward the lunch area, Sammie took her place beside me. I loved walking next to her. We were always perfectly in sync. Like my dad says, we're two halves of the same circle.

"You want to tell me what it is?" she said softly.

Yes, I did. I wanted to tell her everything, to tell her how the whole group was counting on me to do something I knew in my heart was wrong. But I had made a promise, and I keep my promises.

"I can't, it's a secret."

"Since when do we have secrets from each other?"

"Since today." Wow, that was a sad thing to admit. The SF2 secret had now officially come between me and my sister.

We stepped out of the building, and the sun hit me in the face. The morning fog had burned off, and it was another perfect California beach day . . . sunny and clear with a salty tang in the sea air. It took my eyes a second to adjust to the bright light, and in that second, something wonderful happened. I bumped smack into Spencer Ballard. I mean, a full-body bump.

"Just the person I was looking for," he said, picking up my English notebook, which had dropped to the ground. I prayed that it hadn't flipped open to the page where I had written his name in pink and green markers and drawn a pink heart all around it.

"Hey, Sammie, nice to see you, too," he added, giving her a mini fist-bump.

Sammie got a little flustered and actually reached up to tuck her messy hair behind her ears. We both think Spencer is the cutest guy in seventh grade. There are a lot of boys in her Truth Tellers group, but there isn't one who has a dimple like Spencer's.

"Listen, Charlie, we'll be heading off now," Sammie said. "Come find us at our table if you want." I knew what she was doing, and it was so sweet of her. She didn't want to be in the way if Spencer decided to say whatever it is you say when you really like a girl.

Spencer and I watched her and her friends walk away and then stood there awkwardly for a long minute. It was awkward for me, anyway.

"Why were you looking for me?" I asked him finally.

"I was thinking maybe you'd sit with me at lunch," he said. "I have something I want to talk to you about."

The minute I heard those words, I realized what this was about. My heart sank. I bet Sean and the General and Brooke had told him to find me, have lunch with me, and convince me to steal the test. They knew I liked Spencer, and they were using him as their secret weapon. That was low.

"Let's go sit on the grass," he suggested. "I have two granola bars. If you're good, I'll let you have one."

We walked over to a patch of grass under the palm trees. Usually, the grass area is unofficially reserved for eighth-graders, but it was pretty empty today.

"Most of the eighth-graders are at Lincoln," Spencer explained. "They're having an exhibition soccer match. Lots of kids went."

"Sammie and I are going there tomorrow," I said, "to play an exhibition match with the girls' tennis team."

"Maybe I'll come watch you guys. If that's okay with you."

I wanted to jump up and down and do the splits, but instead, I just shrugged and said, "Sure. Whatever."

He pulled two chocolate chip granola bars from his backpack and flipped me one. He whistled as I reached out and caught it.

"Nice reflexes," he said.

We unwrapped our granola bars and each took a bite. When I couldn't stand the silence anymore, I spoke up.

"I know what you want to talk about," I said.

"You do?"

I nodded. "The thing with Lauren, right?"

"You mean that her dad is going to ground her, and she's going to miss Ben's bar mitzvah? It sucks, but why would I want to talk about that with you?"

"Because of the test thing."

"What test thing?"

I looked at him closely, checking for signs that he

was faking. But he was busy chomping down the rest of his granola bar and seemed completely unaware of what I was referring to.

"What test thing?" he repeated, his eyes searching mine to figure out what I was saying. Those were innocent eyes, and I could tell from the look on his face that Spencer wasn't in on the plan. So what were we doing here on the grass? What did he want to talk to me about?

"It's nothing," I lied. "I'm just going to help Lauren study for the history test, that's all."

"Good," he said. "She could use the help. I love Lauren, but studying hard isn't her thing. She's not like you. You've got everything going for you—you're good at school and you're pretty, too. Not to mention that you can smack a tennis ball like a pro."

He laughed and then put the granola bar down. I saw him wipe his hand on his jeans. Then he reached out and put his hand on top of mine.

"What I wanted to say, Charlie, is that I'm really glad you're becoming part of the group," he said without even a trace of embarrassment. "It's great hanging out with you. I'd like to spend more time with you."

Everything faded into the distance . . . Lauren, the test, the teachers' lounge, the conversation with Brooke and the General. The only thing that I was aware of was this moment on the grass, with Spencer's hand on top of mine.

"Are you coming to the game tomorrow night?" he asked.

"I'd like to," I said, trying to make my voice not shake with excitement.

"We all sit together," he said, his dimple popping up from the folds of his cheek. "It's really fun. And then we go out for pizza afterward. It'd be great if you could hang with me. Is that cool with you, Charlie?"

It took everything I had not to scream.

As I sat there with the sun beating down on the back of my neck, my head was swimming and my heart was fluttering. I didn't know what was right or wrong, up or down, true or false, on or off. I only knew one thing for sure: This was the most wonderful moment of my entire life.

The Decision

....

Chapter 5

"I already feel like I'm in prison," Lauren groaned, "and I haven't even been grounded yet."

We were sitting on the Sporty Forty deck after school that day, soaking our feet in the Jacuzzi. Lauren's mom had come to the beach for her daily two-mile jog, and Lauren came along to hang out with me. Sammie says that Lauren hangs out at the club after school because she's hoping Ryan will notice her, but that's not true. She's coming to be with me. As far as I'm concerned, there's a touch of jealousy in Sammie's constant criticism of Lauren.

"You don't know for sure you're going to get grounded," I told Lauren, trying to be reassuring. "You have to think positive. Believe that you're going to ace that test. I could help you study now if you want."

Lauren shook her head. "I just want to hang out now. Besides, we both know it would take a miracle for me to pass."

"Miracles happen. Who knows? The answers to the test could drop out of the sky and land in your lap."

Lauren gave me a funny look.

"That's a weird thing to say," she commented. "You've been drinking too much diet root beer. I think it's rotting your brain."

In fact, it was a weird thing to say if you didn't know that the group was talking about getting her the test in advance. I wished I was like Lauren and didn't know a thing about that plan. I had been thinking about it all afternoon. That is, when I wasn't thinking about Spencer Ballard's dimple and his hand that made my hand smell a little like chocolate chips.

I wiggled my toes in the Jacuzzi, putting my feet right in front of a strong jet of water. I let the stream of water pound them until they tingled. That felt great—in thirty seconds, my feet suddenly felt rested and relaxed. I wished the rest of me felt that way. I had been having an ongoing debate with myself all afternoon and my head was spinning from it. I wanted to be a good friend and help Lauren out, that was for sure. But every time I thought of stealing that test, my conscience spoke up and said, *You know better, Charlie Diamond.* That debate was giving me a giant headache. I wish they had Jacuzzis for your brain.

"Ready or not, here we come," Sammie yelled

from inside the house. With a bang, the screen door flew open and out she came, pushing GoGo in her wheelchair. That maniac actually spun her around on the back wheels a few times before they came to a stop next to the Jacuzzi. We all laughed—except Lauren.

"Your sister's a nutcase," she said, only half joking. I don't think there's a lot of wheelchair spinning at the Wadsworth house.

"Sammie's a wonderfully spontaneous girl," GoGo said, catching her breath. "It's a quality we all should aspire to have."

GoGo was looking very cute today in her big tortoiseshell sunglasses and straw sun hat with a leopard scarf tied around the brim. She was in a great mood because the doctor had told her she could get her cast off on Monday, and even though she'd have to do a lot of physical therapy, she'd be able to move around. Leave it to GoGo to already be planning how to decorate her crutches so they'd be a fashion accessory.

"I hate to break up your party," Sammie said to me, "but it's your turn to take GoGo for her walk."

"Oh, we can skip the walk today," GoGo said. "Charlie and Lauren are having such a nice time. I love how close you girls have become."

The screen door slammed again, and Ryan came sauntering out, his volleyball knee pads around his ankles. He was gobbling a banana in one hand and holding an apple in the other.

"Only animals eat with two hands," Sammie commented.

"Animals and guys returning from volleyball practice," he said. "I worked up a major appetite. You try spiking the ball for an hour straight."

"You're so athletic, Ry," Lauren said. I noticed that she had taken her feet out of the Jacuzzi and was drying them off. Her toenails were painted flaming-hot pink, which looked great with her tan skin.

"You know what, Charlie," she said as she slipped on her matching hot-pink flip-flops. "I think you should take your grandma for her walk. I'd feel terrible if she had to miss it because of me. Maybe Ryan can keep me company while you're gone."

"How convenient," Sammie said. I shot her a *stop-it* look, but she chose to ignore it. Actually, for once I didn't mind leaving Lauren and Ryan together. I was eager to go for a walk with GoGo. My brain was in turmoil, and I needed to talk things through. GoGo is always the person Sammie and I turn to, especially with our mom away in Boston. GoGo never lectures me, but I always feel better after I talk to her.

I pushed her out onto the boardwalk and headed south toward the Santa Monica Pier. It was late in the afternoon, the time when the brown pelicans always come out to fish. A flock of them circled low over the water, their eyes darting back and forth. Then suddenly one of them got straight as an arrow, broke off from the others, and dived headfirst into the ocean.

GoGo and I stopped to watch the show. At first, it disappeared into the water, but when it came up, we knew it'd caught something. You could tell because you could see a big bulge in the pouch under its bill.

"A wonderful bird is the pelican, its bill will hold more than its belican," GoGo said with her usual laugh. She's been saying that poem since we were little, and yet Sammie and I never get tired of it. I think it's because her blue eyes sparkle so much when she recites it. GoGo gets a big kick out of everything, including herself.

"No laugh today?" she asked me. "Not even a smile? Things must be serious, Charlie."

"I have a big decision to make, GoGo. A hard one."

"And let me guess. You can't tell me what it is."

See what I mean? GoGo just knows stuff without even asking.

"I promised my friends I'd keep it a secret."

"A promise between friends is sacred," she said. "Friendship is based on trust, and you can't violate that."

"GoGo, did you ever do anything that you felt was wrong?"

"Of course I did, honey. It's called being alive."

"And did you regret it afterward?"

GoGo sighed. "Regret isn't a very useful emotion, my darling child. It doesn't get you anywhere. But I've tried to learn from my mistakes. That's the best we humans can do."

GoGo turned her wheelchair around to look at me. She reached out and took my hands in hers.

"You're really struggling with this, whatever it is," she said. "I can see that."

"I just don't want to let my friends down, GoGo. But I don't want to let myself down, either."

"It's very rare that a decision is clear, one way or the other. But I know you and trust you'll make the one that feels best."

There was nothing more to say, so we just watched the sky turn that purplish tint it gets before the sun sets. I looked out at the ocean, tracking another flock of pelicans. They were flying in a line with a lead bird out in front. Somehow, they made me think of my friends in the SF2s. We're like a flock, too, with Lauren out in front. Like those birds, we protect one another from harm, help one another out when we're in trouble, stick together no matter what. If I was truly one of them, didn't I owe it to them to be loyal to the flock?

"Charlie, Charlie!" My thoughts were interrupted by Lauren calling me. She was running down the boardwalk toward us, holding her flip-flops in one hand and her cell phone in the other. She was out of breath when she got to us, but she shoved the phone into my hand.

"It's Spencer," she said. "He wants to talk to you. I think you're going to like this conversation. No, make that *love* it!"

"Hello," I said, covering my free ear with my hand to try to block out the sound of the crashing waves.

"Hey, Charlie. It's Spence. I was just talking to Lauren, and she said she was with you. Lucky her."

I just stood there, grinning like an idiot, until I realized that GoGo was observing me closely.

"Nice to talk to you, too, Spencer," I stammered self-consciously.

"So, my dad is going to the game tomorrow night," he went on. "He's on the city council and all, so he loves to be there to shake anyone's hand he can."

"That's nice of him."

"Yeah, well it helps him get reelected, too. Anyhow, he's driving me and Lauren, so she thought it'd be cool if we could pick you up and drive together. How about if we come by the club at six thirty tomorrow? We could take Ryan, too."

I looked over at Lauren. Her grin was as big as mine.

"Say yes," she whispered. "It's like a real double date."

I nodded my head to Lauren, then got back to Spencer. "That sounds fine," I told him. "I'll have to check with my dad, but I think he'll let me go."

"I hate to leave your sister out ..."

"That's okay. She isn't into football games. Besides, I'm sure she's got other plans."

That was only half true. The true part was that Sammie isn't into football games. The not-true part was that I wasn't sure if she had other plans. But she would have to understand. I mean, this was Spencer. And she knew how I felt about him.

"Cool, Charlie. So we're all set," he said. "Listen, I've got to go study. Big history midterm next week, you know."

Did he have to remind me of that test? Just when everything was so perfect?

The minute I hung up, Lauren threw her arms around me.

"This is just like I dreamed it would be," she said, hugging me so hard I actually exhaled involuntarily. "Isn't it great to be best friends?"

"Sounds like you girls have brewed up an exciting weekend," GoGo said.

"Oh, GoGo, you have no idea!" I answered.

"I think I do, Noodle. I'm not so old that I can't remember what a Friday night football game with a special boy feels like."

"Your grandma's the coolest," Lauren said, reaching out and planting a kiss on GoGo's cheek.

"You're a sweet girl, Lauren."

Yes, she was. I loved the way she treated GoGo. And Lauren was so happy for me, just like a best friend is supposed to be. GoGo was so happy for me. I was so happy for me.

I know you'll make the decision that feels best, GoGo had said.

And right then and there as I watched that flock

of pelicans flying in a perfect, unified formation in the sky above us—each one a part of a group that depended on the others for survival—I knew my decision was made.

The Teachers' Lounge

....

Chapter 6

"Charlie, I can't find my Beachside tennis shorts and sweatshirt," Sammie hollered into the bathroom.

I was in the shower letting the hot water pound on my back and trying to wake up. I hadn't slept well all night. I kept having this dream, a nightmare really. In it, I had two faces. One of them was happy and smiling and blowing kisses to a crowd of people I couldn't see, like the way Miss America or a prom queen does after she's crowned. But when that face turned around, there was another one on the back side. This one was stern and angry like Ms. Daily, the sour biddy who was vice principal at our old school and was always shaking her head at me like I'd done something really wrong. Every hour, I'd wake myself up trying to get those two faces out of my head, and each time I fell back to sleep, there they were again.

"Did you hear me?" Sammie yelled, pushing open the bathroom door. "I've searched our closet and every drawer."

"They're in your tennis bag," I called out. "I packed them for you. And close the door, you're letting all the steam out."

We were playing with the girls' tennis team in the exhibition match at Lincoln after school, but Sammie is so scattered, I knew she'd forget to bring her tennis outfit. It's always up to me to remember everything. Maybe that's why I'm tense. Half the time, I feel like my shoulders are up around my ears. The only thing that helps is to stand in the shower and let the steamy water relax my tight muscles.

That morning, I wished I could stay in the shower forever. I had a big day in front of me, and all of it was making me nervous. The tennis match. The football game with Spencer. And, oh yeah, the thing in the teachers' lounge. That's how I had come to think of it. The "thing in the teachers' lounge."

After a few more minutes in the shower, when the tips of my fingers were good and wrinkly, I got out and dried my hair. Lots of days, I don't actually blow it dry, but today was special, and I wanted my hair to be straight and shiny like Lauren's hair always looks.

Both Sammie and I were running late, so my dad agreed to drive us to school. We pulled up in the carpool lane just in time, right behind a black Lexus that belonged to the General's dad. As soon as he pulled away and the General was out on the sidewalk, I opened my door, grabbed my tennis gear, and piled out.

"See you, Dad," Sammie said.

"Come see us play," I added.

"I'll try," he called out. "Go easy today. Save your good stuff for the tournament on Sunday."

Sammie's homeroom is in the bungalows, which meant she had to dash off so she wouldn't be late. I ran up the steps to the main building. Inside, the General was waiting for me by the door. Ms. Carew, our English teacher, was posting a notice about a poetry contest on the bulletin board nearby.

"Big day today," the General said to me with a wink.

"*Sshhhh,*" I whispered, pointing at Ms. Carew.

Okay, that was a crazy reaction. Why would she be suspicious of an innocent remark like that? *Don't be so paranoid,* I told myself. As we walked past Ms. Carew, I made myself smile and say hello.

"Nice to see you, Charlie," she said.

She was one of the few teachers who could always

tell Sammie and me apart. Even though Sammie is chunkier than I am, we still look a lot alike. Most of the other teachers don't remember which one is which so they just say hi without a name. We're used to that, though.

The General dropped me off at Ms. Hamel's homeroom, where I didn't hear a word she said. I was in the same state of jittery nerves the whole morning. First-period math dragged on forever, as did second-period Spanish. Señora Molina taught us to sing "La Bamba," which ordinarily might have been fun, but I was too nervous to enjoy it. I was worried my voice would shake when I sang.

I was not even a little bit hungry at lunch. To be honest, I was actually kind of nauseous, not the sick kind, but the kind you get when you're really nervous. Instead of eating, I arranged with Sammie to go into the girls' bathroom and change into our tennis outfits. The bus was taking us to Lincoln right after school, and we wouldn't have time to change. As I pulled my hair back into a ponytail and smoothed all the loose ends behind my red headband, I noticed Sammie staring at me in the mirror.

"What?" I said.

"Your hands are shaking."

"So what? I'm a little nervous about this match."

"It's just an exhibition match, Charlie. For fun."

"That sweatshirt looks good on you," I said, changing the subject.

"Yeah, it's nice and big so it covers the stomach flab."

"Don't put yourself down, Sammie. You look cute."

"Then so do you, bubble brain. We're wearing exactly the same thing."

I had just enough time to help Sammie with her hair before the bell rang. We always wear ponytails and headbands for a match. *Keeps the hair out of the face,* Dad says. Sammie is notoriously sloppy about getting all her hair pulled back, so I put a little water on my hands and smoothed her hair back before I slipped the red headband onto her head.

"Meet you at the flagpole after school," I said as we left the bathroom.

"Charlie, we're going to English together. It's not like you won't see me. What's wrong with you, anyway?"

"Nothing," I answered, trying to cover up my nervousness. "Just remember to bring your tennis bag for the match."

"Anyone ever tell you you're a nag?" she said.

"Yeah, you."

I practically jumped out of my skin during fifth-period English. I wanted this teachers' lounge thing over with already. I had decided I would just do it and then never have to think about it again. A flood of relief swept over me when sixth period came and I headed to Mr. Newhart's history class. Soon it would all be over. Both Brooke and the General were waiting for me outside the door. So was Ben Feldman, who isn't even in our class.

"Stopping by for support," he whispered to me. "Brooke told me about it. And just to say thanks, I'm going to put your picture up on the big screen at Dodger Stadium that night. Your face is going to be thirty feet high in full-color Diamond vision."

"Thanks, Ben. That's so nice of you."

"Well, to be honest, we're doing it for everyone." He grinned. "But I just wanted to give you something cool to look forward to."

Lily March is in our history class, too, and when she saw me in the hall, she just smiled and said she liked my headband. I was a little self-conscious wearing all my tennis gear in class, but to tell the truth, I was glad to be wearing that big sweatshirt. It's really loose on me and would cover . . . well . . . cover anything that might be under it, if you know what I mean. I searched Lily's face for a sign that she knew what was about to happen, but she just took off her vintage tie-dyed scarf and slid into her seat.

Lauren came dashing in just as I was taking my seat. I sit right in front of the General. That's because Mr. Newhart seats everyone alphabetically. Diamond ... Dickerson ... you get the picture. Lauren sits in the next-to-the-last seat in the last row because she's a *W*. Only Melissa Zachary is behind her. I glanced in their direction as the bell rang. Melissa had her notebook open and was already marking her class notes with a yellow highlighter. Lauren had her notebook open, too, but I could see that hardly anything was written down. I've seen her notes before. All they have are her doodles of sunglasses. She wants to be a sunglasses designer when she grows up, which is why she believes she shouldn't be required to know Egyptian history. Those Egyptians didn't even wear sunglasses, she claims.

Mr. Newhart is nice, but a really hard grader. He loves history, and when he teaches, he gets so excited about the subject that sometimes he even acts it out. He's famous at Beachside for wearing a toga and sandals when he teaches Roman history. We haven't seen that because we're still on Egypt and probably won't get to Rome until January.

He didn't waste any time getting started after the bell rang. Clearly, he was in a serious mood. It was review day for our midterm, and he announced that he would spend a half hour going over the notes in detail. After that, he'd devote the rest of the period to answering all our last-minute questions.

During the review session, I had a little trouble breathing. I wasn't choking or anything, I just felt like

I couldn't take a deep breath. I tried to do a little of the yoga breathing my dad had taught us to settle our nerves before a big match. It helped somewhat.

When the half hour was up and Mr. Newhart called for questions, Brooke looked over at me and mouthed the word *now*. I put my hand up, but lost courage before it was all the way in the air. Mr. Newhart called on Josh Otto instead, who asked about where the boundary was between the Upper Kingdom and the Lower Kingdom. While Mr. Newhart drew a map of Egypt on the board, the General passed me a note written in green ink that said, *You're next.* It had a green arrow pointing to the front of the class. I crumpled it up and stuck it in my sweatshirt pocket.

"Who else has a question?" Mr. Newhart asked.

The General poked me in the back, and my hand shot up into the air.

"Yes, Ms. Diamond."

"This isn't exactly about Egypt," I began. My voice sounded weird to me as if it was bouncing off the walls and coming back into my ears. No one else seemed to notice. "Um . . . could I have a bathroom pass, please?"

A few boys in the back of the room snickered. Mr. Newhart didn't lose a beat giving them a menacing stare at the same time as he handed me the wooden hall pass. His attention immediately turned to both Brooke and the General, who were raising their hands urgently and calling his name.

"I have a question, I have a question," they both said at once. Just like they promised, they had my back.

As I left, I heard Brooke asking, "So what's the deal with King Tut dying when he was still a teenager? Did he do drugs or something?"

I slipped into the hall, looked around, and breathed a sigh of relief. It was empty. Quickly, I tiptoed to the open door of the teachers' lounge. I stuck my head in. No one was there, so I darted inside and closed the door. It was half the size of a classroom, with a couple of couches, some orange plastic chairs, a computer on the desk, and a huge copy machine. At the far end of the room was a half-open door. I assumed it was the closet with the files.

I walked toward it quickly and went inside. Five metal file cabinets lined the wall. I picked one and counted three drawers down. The plastic blue label on the front said *NEWHART*. I slid the drawer open, hoping it wouldn't make a noise. It was quiet, just a tiny rolling sound as the drawer glided along its tracks.

The drawer was jam-packed with folders hanging from a small rod. Each folder was neatly labeled with a plastic tab. They said things like *Ancient Civilization Pop Quiz, Roman Empire Essay Questions, Greek Philosophers Unit Test.* Then I saw it, halfway back in the drawer.

Egypt Unit Midterm.

My heart was beating so fast I thought it was going to fly out of my chest and take off for Mars.

I put my hand on the file and pried it open. Inside there were probably fifty copies of the test. It was a thick stack. Mr. Newhart would never notice one was missing. I reached my hand into the file and tugged on one of the stapled tests. Then I stopped.

In my mind, I saw the stern, angry face from my dream.

"What are you doing, Charlie?" she said. "You can't do this. You don't steal."

Suddenly, that face was gone, and the smiling face blowing kisses popped up.

"But Lauren's your best friend," she said. "She even said so. She needs your help."

I stood there in the closet, frozen in fear. The clock on the wall clicked as the minute hand moved forward. I had to decide quickly. It was dangerous to stay there any longer.

With a deep breath, I closed my eyes, plunged my hand into the file and pulled out a test. I didn't even look at it. I didn't want to see it. Shaking like a leaf, I stuffed the paper under my sweatshirt and slid the drawer closed. In two giant leaps, I was across the room and at the door. Checking to make sure the paper was securely hidden and tucked into my shorts, I opened the door and stepped out into the hall.

No one was there. I had done it.

I walked shakily to the water fountain, took a long drink, and even splashed some of the cool water on my sweating face. I don't usually sweat. Sammie is the sweater.

Sammie. What would she think of me now? What would she say if she knew what I had done?

In a flash, it all became clear to me. I couldn't go through with it. I had to return the test. It wasn't me doing this. It wasn't the Charlie Diamond I knew.

I turned to cross the hall, to go back into the teachers' lounge. I was so crazed with guilt and fear that I didn't see the figure coming toward me and smacked right into someone. I gasped.

"It's okay, sweetie. It's just me."

It was Brooke, coming out of Mr. Newhart's room, carrying her big designer purse with all the gold buckles hanging off it.

"What are you doing here?" I whispered.

"Bathroom pass," she said. "I sort of implied that I had my period. It works every time."

Before I could say anything, she reached out and touched my sweatshirt. The test paper crinkled underneath.

"Way to go," she giggled. And in one swift movement, she grabbed the paper from me and stuffed it into her purse. "We'll get this to Lauren. And don't worry, you'll get the credit for doing it."

Then, without another word, she trotted off to the girls' bathroom.

I stood in the hall trying to recover. It was done. Out of my hands now. There was nothing I could do. History had been written, and I couldn't go back and rewrite it now.

Smoothing my hair and taking a deep breath, I headed back to Mr. Newhart's class. Everything looked normal. The gardener was trimming the hedges just outside the door. The California flag was waving in the sea breeze. Students were sitting at their desks, taking notes, and writing down homework assignments. It was just another day at Beachside Middle School.

Everything was going to be all right.

The Game

....

Chapter 7

"We're here, Cinderella!" Lauren called from the porch. "Your pumpkin coach awaits you."

I spit the toothpaste into the bathroom sink and checked myself out in the mirror. I had put on a little mascara, and Lauren had loaned me her new pale-purple eye shadow. She said it would make my eyes look brighter blue than they already are. She was right. I was happy with the way I looked. My cheeks were still rosy from the tennis match, where Sammie and I played several great sets. Actually, Sammie played great—I was just okay. I was still shaky from the teachers' lounge thing and my reflexes were way off, but Sammie covered for all my mistakes. Spencer came to see us, and after we won, he proclaimed us the "awesome twosome."

I hurried out of the bathroom and found Lauren in the living room talking to Dad and GoGo. Ryan was shoving in a last-minute taco at the kitchen counter just in case he couldn't get enough food at the game. Sammie was sprawled on the couch, eating a tangerine.

"Who are you playing tonight?" my dad was asking Lauren.

"Lincoln Middle School."

"I bet they're plenty intimidated after the way my girls whipped them today in the tennis match," he bragged.

"*One* of your girls," Ryan observed. "The other one seemed a little distracted. Right, Charles?"

"None of that on Sunday," my dad said, giving me the big stink eye. "In tournament play, there's no room for distraction."

"Yeah, you'd better get your game face on," Ryan warned, popping the last of the taco in his mouth and coming to join Lauren. She didn't seem to mind that he had a few shreds of lettuce still hanging off his lower lip. If he were my date, I'd mind for sure.

"Well, tonight Charlie has her party face on," GoGo said. "And she looks lovely."

"Come on, you two." Lauren grabbed my hand and headed for the door. I noticed she grabbed Ryan's hand, too. "Spencer and his dad are waiting in the car."

"Sammie, aren't you going?" GoGo asked.

"Nope. I have plans."

"She and I are watching some tennis videos," my dad explained. "She's got some work to do if she wants to improve her second serve."

That seemed like a rotten evening, and I felt bad for Sammie. I thought at least she'd have something fun planned with Alicia or Sara.

"You can come with us, Sammie," I offered. Okay, I'll admit it. I didn't sound very convincing. It was a halfhearted offer at best, and she knew it.

"Come on," Ryan urged, with more enthusiasm than I had managed to muster. "Bring your tangerine. Bring two. Let's make it a party."

"There's no time," Lauren said, heading out the door and yanking us out after her. "We've really got to hurry. Next time you can go with us, Sammie. Promise."

And just like that, we were in the driveway and climbing into Spencer's dad's car.

"Hey, Diamond kids. Great to see you," Mr. Ballard said in his big, booming voice as he rolled down his driver's side window. "One of you up front, the others in back."

"My legs and I will take the front," Ryan said. He's tall for his age, which helps in volleyball but means he's always squinched up like a pretzel when we're in the backseat of the car. I could see that Lauren was disappointed about the seat arrangement. No doubt she was counting on cuddling up close to him in the backseat. But she was really nice and let me go in the middle next to Spencer. I confess, I was pretty happy at the idea of being squished up next to him.

As we drove to the school and Mr. Ballard rambled on about how he thinks sports are the answer to society's problem with young people, I thought I felt Spencer's arm drape around me and land on my shoulder. Was it intentional, or was it just too crowded in the backseat and he needed a place for his arm? I glanced over at him, and he raised his eyebrows at me in a playful little gesture. From that adorable move, I knew that it was intentional.

Sometimes, life is just that good.

The football game was even more fun than I had imagined. Because Ryan was with us, we sat with the eighth-graders and no one even teased us about being seventh-grade punks. During the first half, a few more of our group joined us—Brooke and the General, Sean and Jillian and a baseball player named Dan White, who, Lauren says, has a crush on me. He's really nice and all, but let's face it, he's missing a dimple. My entire group seemed glad to be sitting with the eighth-graders, and I was happy that us Diamonds could bring them that kind of status.

At halftime, Lauren and I went to the bathroom. It

was the first time we had been alone together all day.

"You are the best friend any girl could ever have," she gushed the minute we got inside. "I know what you did for me today, Charlie, and I want you to know I'll never forget it."

Two girls were washing their hands in the sink near us, and I saw them look up. Naturally, they were curious about what I had done that was so unforgettable.

"Let's talk about this another time," I whispered to Lauren.

"Oh, right." She nodded. The girls lost interest, dried their hands, and left. As soon as they were gone, she whispered to me again. "Listen, I was thinking, do you maybe want to come over and study for the history test with me tomorrow? I have something we can both share."

She giggled. Suddenly, I felt so ashamed—even though no one was there to hear or see anything.

"Lauren," I said. "I don't want to see the test. I don't want to know about it. I feel bad enough that I took it. So let's just forget it and move on, okay?"

"I thought you wanted to get it for me. For us."

"I did it for you, Lauren. Not for me."

Before she could answer, a group of girls from Lincoln came in. They were all wearing their school colors, purple and white, and were talking excitedly about the game. When they saw me, they giggled.

"Hey, aren't you that tennis player?" one of them

said, looking at me in the mirror. "The one with the identical sister?"

"That's me. We played at your school today."

"Yeah, you guys rock. I've always wanted to know . . . do twins have the same thoughts and everything?"

I laughed. That question didn't bother me because Sammie and I get it all the time. People have weird ideas about twins. Some people think we're freaks, and other people get all supernatural about it. For us, it's just who we are and have always been.

"We look alike," I told her, "but we're two very separate people."

I thought about my answer as Lauren and I walked back to the field. Sometimes Sammie and I actually do have the same thoughts. We both love sushi and hate asparagus. We both cry at exactly the same places in sad movies. We both say *gesundheit* after anyone sneezes and *jinx* when two people say the same word at the same time. And we share pretty much the same beliefs about family and friends and stuff. At least we did up until today. I couldn't stop wondering if Sammie would have done the same thing I did for one of her friends. I bet she would do anything for Alicia, too. Wouldn't she?

Sammie was in my thoughts, too, when we went out for pizza after the game. Mr. Ballard ordered two large sausage and mushroom pizzas, which is the kind Sammie and I always share. After the first piece, I excused myself and went to the bathroom, closed the door to the last stall, and called her.

"Hey, party girl," she answered.

"How's your night, Sammie?"

"Couldn't be better. Dad and I had a fascinating discussion about racket positions. Then we did some footwork drills. It's a real party atmosphere here."

"I wish you had come with us."

"Thanks, but we both know I'm not the football type."

I heard the bathroom door swish open.

"Charlie? You in here?" Lauren called.

"Be right out!" I hollered back. "Listen, I have to go," I whispered into the phone.

"Okay. But you have to swear to me, Charlie. If you kiss that hot Spencer, you have to tell me everything, okay?"

Sammie and I had always promised each other that whoever got kissed first would describe every detail, no holding back. So far, neither of us had.

If you're wondering if Spencer kissed me when he dropped me off back at the club after pizza, the answer is no. But he did say that he'd try to stop by the Sand and Surf Club on Sunday and catch some of the tournament. When I said, "Wow, you're turning into a real tennis fan," he whispered back, "And a Charlie fan, too."

I don't know if that was better than a kiss, but it was right up there.

All day Saturday, I alternated between studying for my midterm and practicing for the tournament. If it were up to my dad, he'd have us working out all day every day because our tennis is the most important thing to him. We just got our ranking in the Under-14 Doubles category, and his goal is for us to be in the top ten in the state. Then we'd be assured college scholarships. My mom is more into our academics, and when she left for cooking school, she made GoGo promise that she'd see to it that we kept up with our studies. So when I wasn't on the court with Dad, GoGo quizzed me about Egypt.

"You know a lot about these guys," I told her, slurping down a slice of the juicy honeydew melon she had carved up for us.

"The Egyptians had a fascinating culture," she said. "I studied them when I was learning to make jewelry. Do you know they made some of the most beautiful golden body decorations ever?"

Then we googled Egyptian jewelry and looked

at the rings and bracelets and even pure-gold masks they made. I liked it so much that after dinner, I spent the whole night reading about ancient Egypt.

When I was in our room reading, Sammie asked if Alicia could sleep over. My dad said no, just as I thought he would. It was one of his rules: No sleepovers the night before a tournament. We had to get our rest. So Sammie just had some lean protein (that's my dad's word for chicken breasts) for dinner, then hung around and watched TV. During one of my reading breaks, I tried calling Lauren to review our double date, but her mom said she had gone to the mall with Jillian and then was sleeping over. I was surprised that she was out all day. She said she was going to spend the day studying for history. I mean, even if you have the test, you still have to look up the answers and memorize them.

Our tournament was being held at the Sand and Surf Tennis Club, which is a couple of miles up Pacific Coast Highway from the Sporty Forty. It's a deluxe, old-school place with a mahogany wood lounge and red leather chairs and a snack bar that serves iced Cokes in real glasses and the best sweet potato fries ever. Because they have ten tennis courts that are brand-new, it's where the Tennis Association holds their big satellite tournaments.

The fog was just burning off when we arrived at the Sand and Surf Sunday morning at ten. Dad parked the car while Sammie and I went to register. Ryan was coming later. He was going to jog down the beach after volleyball practice and watch our afternoon match.

"Don't want to miss out on those sweet potato fries," he'd said as we left. "I'm ordering a double humongous basket."

"Why don't you ask them to throw them in a trough, and you can snort them down like a pig?" Sammie said.

"Excellent idea, Sam. I'll stop at the hardware store and pick up a trough on my way over."

You can't insult Ryan. He has a comeback for everything.

When we registered, we found out that our first match was against Caroline Huang and Erin Knight from the Los Angeles Racquet Club. We had played them before, and they had beaten us, so we knew they were solid players. But we both felt that we had improved since then, and if we were really on our game, we could beat them this time. We weren't scheduled to begin until eleven fifteen, so even after we warmed up, we still had a half hour to sit in the lounge and wait for our court time. I pulled out my phone and checked my texts. There was one from Lauren.

Bought you something in the mall last
night. To say thanks to my new BFF.

"Thanks for what?" I heard Sammie's voice say. I jumped so high I almost dropped my phone. I spun around in my chair, and there she was, hanging over my shoulder staring at my phone.

"Since when do you read my texts?" I snapped.

"Since when do you have secrets?" she snapped back.

"Sammie, we're about to play a big match. We have to focus."

"I am focused, Charlie. You're the one who's been all spacey the last couple of days. What's going on, anyway? I can feel something's not right."

"Everything's fine. I just have a lot on my mind."

Sammie looked me in the eyes. I don't know if it was one of those "twin moments" people talk about. Maybe it was. But she could tell I was lying.

"If something's wrong or if you're in some kind of trouble, you can always talk to me," she said. "I love you, and I'm here for you."

I felt my eyes well up with tears. She had no idea how much I wanted to tell her what was wrong. How my life was changing so fast. How confused I was about everything. How much I felt I was leaving her behind. How much I wanted to share everything with her, even borrowing the test, the thing I had done that I was most ashamed of.

"Diamond and Diamond versus Huang and Knight," the voice on the loudspeaker called out. "Report to court eight."

This was no time for tears, and certainly no time for confessions. It was time to put on our game faces.

The Test

....

Chapter 8

"You girls played great in the first match," Dad said the next morning while toasting our whole wheat waffles for breakfast. He always reviews our matches for at least several days after a tournament, replaying them in his head. That's how obsessed he is. "I was impressed the way you took Huang and Knight to the cleaners. You were all business out there."

Sammie and I had been in total sync for that first set. I'm quicker, so I play net. She's strong, so she plays back. And the combination worked perfectly against Huang and Knight. We were on fire, or as Ryan says, *"En fuego."*

But my dad couldn't leave it at that.

"Charlie, what happened to you in the afternoon? You lost focus."

He didn't have to tell me. For the second match, Sammie and I drew Kimberly McCall and Nicole Dennis, who we've played before. They're from the Malibu Racquet Club, and they're tough competitors. We were holding our own, though, and were tied at one set apiece, until you-know-who got all fuzzy in the head. I can tell you the minute it happened. It was when Ryan arrived, and I saw him climbing into the stands, holding a huge bag of sweet potato fries. That wasn't what did it, though. I'm used to Ryan creating a scene. It was who he was with that shook me up.

Lauren.

What was she doing there?

I'll tell you what. Hanging out with Ryan. Munching on sweet potato fries. Looking fabulous in a powder-blue Juicy tracksuit. Cheering for me. The only thing she wasn't doing was preparing for the history midterm, which I went through a lot of pain to help her with. That thought was pretty distracting to me.

A little while later, Spencer arrived. He waved and sat down in the stands to watch us play. Talk about losing focus! His being there was the finishing blow to any shred of focus I might have had. Good-bye, net shot. Hello, Spencer. Every time I glanced up, all I saw was his cute dimple.

I probably don't have to tell you that we lost that match. It wasn't totally my fault; Sammie's play was off, too. She doesn't like it when Lauren comes to watch us, because she thinks she's there to see Ryan and not really to root for us. But as I've mentioned before, Sammie's got a jealousy problem when it comes to Lauren, even though she'd be the last person to admit it.

"So this week we intensify your practice schedule," Dad was saying, handing us each a waffle to eat on the way to school. "I want you girls out on the court every afternoon."

"I have Truth Tellers Monday after school," Sammie said.

"And I have cheerleading practice."

"I don't care what else you have," he said. "You have to make time for your tennis. That's what's going to pave the road to your future. Diligence and hard work pay off."

I gathered my stuff together, tossed Sammie her backpack, and we bolted out the door before he had a chance to go into lecture number three, the one where he tells us that to be winners and have successful lives, you have to give 110 percent.

"How's your party coming along?" I asked Sammie as we climbed the hill called the "California Incline" that takes us from the beach up to town where school is.

"The plans are temporarily on hold. Alicia had to spend the weekend studying."

"Oh, right. She's got Mr. Newhart for history, too."

"Yeah, third period. Alicia is totally freaked. She

says Mr. Newhart is an impossible grader. She's studying so hard I didn't even talk to her once all weekend."

I didn't answer. Instead, I pretended to be huffing and puffing up the steep hill. I felt more than a twinge of guilt that Alicia was studying so hard while Lauren was partying.

"Anyway," Sammie went on, "Mr. Mintner doesn't care if we know every little detail. He says it's the big picture he's after."

As we neared school, we saw Alicia up ahead. Usually, she looks good when she comes to school. She loves to wear embroidered tops from her native country, El Salvador, and they look really cute with jeans. But this morning, she looked . . . I don't mean to sound judgmental . . . so I'll just say she looked kind of messy. Like the way she looks when she's just hanging out with Sammie. Beat-up hoodie, baggy jeans, running-shoes-with-no-socks type of thing.

"Wow, she's really taking this studying thing seriously," I said to Sammie. "No time to pick a fresh outfit, I guess."

"Not like Lauren Wadsworth who has Esperanza to iron her clothes," Sammie shot back.

"I'm sorry, Sammie," I said. "I deserved that."

I didn't intend to say a mean thing about Alicia. I really do like her.

"Man, I had a terrible weekend," Alicia said as we caught up to her. "My mom had to work late at the

Wadsworths' Saturday to get the house ready for some big party they were having. My grandma has a cold, which means I had to babysit Ramon, who ate a whole box of raisins and then threw them up all over the carpet. It was gross. Remind me never to give raisins to a four-year-old."

"I'll make a mental note of it," Sammie said, and Alicia laughed.

"Don't even ask about Sunday," she went on. "Ramon got his finger caught in the door, and we had to take him to the emergency room to get three stitches. He kept making me kiss his finger all night. Double, triple gross."

"Sounds gross," Sammie said. "Did you get a chance to study for history?"

"Here and there. Not nearly enough. I'll just have to power through that midterm somehow."

"I can study with you at lunch," I offered. "I know the material pretty well."

"Thanks, Charlie. But I have history third period. My fate will be sealed by lunch—for better or for worse. And I'm pretty sure it's going to be for worse."

By the time we got to school, a lot of kids were hanging around on the grass, waiting for the bell to ring. Jillian saw us and came bouncing over.

"Here's everyone's favorite new girl," she said to me. It was clear that Brooke had told her about me getting the test for Lauren.

Sammie gave me a strange look as if to say *Since when did you become everyone's favorite?* Fortunately, good old Jillian didn't pause and just went barreling right on to the next topic.

"Whoa, Alicia," she said. "What's up with the outfit? You auditioning for *World's Dirtiest Jobs?*"

Even though everyone knows that Jillian sees life as one big reality show, I still thought it was a rude remark.

"Yeah, right after you get the lead on *World's Biggest Airhead*," Alicia responded.

"Oh, that would be so cool," Jillian giggled, not quite getting the insult. She'd do anything to be on TV, even be an airhead, which come to think of it, comes pretty naturally to her.

People were heading to class. Sammie and Alicia took off toward the bungalows, and Jillian and I headed up the front stairs. She noticed me looking around.

"Spencer has a dentist appointment this morning," she said.

"What makes you think I was looking for him?"

"You can't hide anything in our group, Charlie. We see it all. Like what you did for Lauren. That's called being a good friend."

I didn't want to talk about it.

"For your information, Jillian, I was actually looking for Lauren, not Spencer."

"Then look no further," a voice said. I whipped around and saw Lauren, who had snuck up on us.

"Where'd you come from?" I asked.

"My dad's BMW. See?" She turned and waved to her father as he drove off. "He lectured me all the way to school, and I didn't say a word because I know that he is going to be so happy with me tomorrow night. Wait till he sees my grade on the midterm. His little girl is going to make him proud. Thanks to you."

She hooked her arm in mine, and the three of us walked into the building.

"Like my new jeans?" she chattered on. "Wait till you see what I got for you, Charlie. You're going to love it. It's for the bar mitzvah."

As we headed down the hall, we passed the teachers' lounge. Mr. Newhart was just coming out, carrying a stack of about fifty stapled papers in a folder. I knew that folder. We had met before. I gulped, and my stomach did a 360.

"Hi, Mr. Newhart," Lauren called out.

"Hello, Ms. Wadsworth. Ready for the exam?"

"I was born ready," Lauren said with a laugh.

"We'll see about that," was all he said.

I ran into Alicia at lunch. She looked a wreck, even worse than in the morning.

"That midterm is a monster," she said. "A fire-breathing monster with claws and fangs. Be warned."

Instead of sitting with my friends at our table at lunch, I went to the library to go over my notes one more time. I think it was the claws and fangs remark that did it. By the end of lunch, I felt like I knew my stuff. GoGo and I had studied well. I could even spell Tutankhamen, which is the full name of King Tut.

I've taken a lot of midterms since I started middle school, but Alicia was right about this one—it was the mother of all midterms. There was matching, multiple choice, true/false, fill in the blank, plus a map of Egypt where you had to draw in all the cities and rivers. You had to know the kings and queens, a whole slew of gods and what they represented, the architecture, the geography, and about a million dates. And for the short-answer part, you had to know how to spell impossible words like *papyrus*, and *hieroglyphics*, and *Nefertiti*.

Everyone in my class groaned all the way through it.

Not Lauren, though. She never looked up from her paper, never groaned, and never erased so much as one letter. She spent the whole period sitting at her desk, concentrating on the work in front of her, checking off answers like the most confident student in the world. Occasionally, I'd sneak a glance at Mr. Newhart as he walked up and down the aisles to see if he was watching her or noticing anything unusual. But he seemed totally normal. Every now and then he'd check his watch and tell us how much time we had left. Most of us were still writing when he called out, "Time's up."

Everyone but Lauren. She was the first one at his desk, putting her test paper down on top of his roll book.

"You look pleased with yourself, Ms. Wadsworth," he said.

"I studied like a fiend this weekend," she said. "I hope it paid off."

"Hard work always does," he said with a nice smile.

I went up to the desk and put my paper on top of Lauren's.

"And you, Ms. Diamond. You look less happy with yourself. I take it you didn't study like a fiend."

"I tried," I said.

"Charlie had to play in a big tennis tournament, too," Lauren explained. "She's a ranked player, you know."

"That's very admirable," Mr. Newhart said. "But there is such a thing as a scholar-athlete. Someone who makes time for sports and studies. You might want to strive for that, Ms. Diamond. I see exceptional potential in you."

The way he looked at me made me extremely uncomfortable. Why was he telling me that? Did he know something? Had he figured out that I helped Lauren cheat? Maybe he was psychic and could read my mind. I read a story in *People* magazine about a psychic schoolteacher. Well, maybe it wasn't a schoolteacher, but it was some kind of psychic.

Stop it, Charlie, I told myself. *You're getting paranoid again. Just smile and say good-bye.*

"Good-bye, Mr. Newhart," I said with a smile. And then I got out of there as fast as I could.

As we walked to our lockers, Lauren suggested that we go to Starbucks after school to celebrate.

"My treat," she said.

"I can't stay long," I told her. "Sammie and I have to practice. Our dad wasn't too happy that we lost yesterday."

"We'll just get one little, tiny Frappuccino," she said. "You can be home in half an hour."

After school, I met Lauren and we walked to Starbucks. She never stopped talking. I thought she was going to float right off the ground. She was so happy.

"You know what, Charlie?" she said. "I think I got

almost everything right. How do you think you did?"

"Probably not as well as you."

"Understandably. You didn't have *you* to help you. I purposely made a few mistakes," she babbled on, "because I didn't want it to look too perfect. For instance, I said Nefertiti was the wife of King Tut, even though I know she was married to Akhenaton, whose mummy, by the way, has never been identified." Then suddenly she stopped walking and burst out laughing. "Listen to me," she said. "I actually learned this material."

In some strange way, that made me feel much better. Yes, I got the test for her. Yes, it was cheating. *But look at the result,* I told myself. Lauren had learned everything she needed to know. She knew as much about Egyptian history as I did. And we were going to get to go to Ben Feldman's bar mitzvah. And our faces would be lit up on a thirty-foot-high screen. Things weren't so bad. In fact, everything had turned out pretty well.

Things got even better the next day when Mr. Newhart returned our test papers. Lauren got a 96 percent, which was a solid A. Not the highest A in the class—that went to Phoebe Lee, of course, Will

Lee's older sister. But Lauren's score would be good enough to get her at least a B-minus in the class. And I surprised myself, too. I got a 94 percent, the highest grade I'd gotten on any of my tests or quizzes so far.

Lauren took me to Starbucks again. We got orange mango smoothies and clinked our plastic glasses together in a toast to us.

"To friendship," she said. "To fun. To the good life."

We took big sips of our delicious smoothies.

I felt happy. Yes, I had gone through some rough moments, but they were over now. There was nothing but great times ahead.

Or at least that's what I thought.

The Principal's Office

....

Chapter 9

"Please report immediately to Principal Pfeiffer's office," the summons read. It was Wednesday, the day after we got our history midterms back, and I was sitting in Señora Molina's second-period Spanish class. A messenger from the office had just delivered the note to me in a sealed envelope.

I held the yellow slip in my hand and read the words over and over.

Please report immediately to Principal Pfeiffer's office.

Ms. Molina's voice was only a dim echo in the distant background, and the whole room was swimming. My mind was racing. Why did Principal Pfeiffer want to see me? What could this mean? Had he found out about the test? No, how could he? No one saw me take it. Maybe it was just a routine summons to go over my classes for next year. No, that would be Ms. King's job, the counselor. Plus it's way too early for that. Well, maybe it was to congratulate me on being such a great new addition to Beachside. To say how proud he was of our new tennis ranking. Or maybe he wanted to ask if I'd give tennis lessons to his son who was in kindergarten. I had seen them a couple of weekends ago, batting around a ball at the Douglas Park public courts.

From deep within the chaos of my thoughts, I heard Señora Molina's voice talking to me.

"Excuse me?" I said.

"Perdón," she corrected.

Really, Señora Molina, this was no time to be a stickler for the Spanish-only rule.

"I was asking you, Carlotta, if everything was all right," Señora Molina said.

"I ... I don't know. I just have to go to the principal's office," I stammered.

"Then you should take your books with you and make sure you call a friend for the homework assignment," she told me.

As I stuffed my Spanish book in my backpack, I wondered why she thought the meeting with Principal Pfeiffer was going to take the whole period. Did she know something I didn't know? Or was I just being paranoid?

Principal Pfeiffer's office was upstairs in the

main building. I had to walk by Mr. Falb's science classroom on the way there. Lauren and Brooke have science second period together, and I was hoping like crazy I could talk to at least one of them for a second. Maybe they could give me a heads-up about why the principal wanted to see me in his office.

The door to Mr. Falb's room was open, so I stuck my head in. He was in the middle of doing an experiment for the class, holding a beaker over a Bunsen burner and saying something about the average mass of an unpopped popcorn kernel. When Lauren saw me, she let out a little squeal and waved. Mr. Falb looked up at her, then at me. He was wearing safety goggles, which made him look like an alien. His eyes looked as if they had popped out of his head, like magnified bug eyes.

"May I help you?" he asked.

"I was wondering if I could talk to Lauren for a second."

"Correct me if I'm mistaken, young lady, but I believe we are in the middle of a class period," he said, his buggy eyes getting even buggier.

I took that as a giant no.

"I was just on my way to Principal Pfeiffer's office," I said in a loud enough voice so Lauren could hear. "But I guess it's a bad time."

Lauren gave me a puzzled look and shrugged. It was clear she didn't know anything more about the summons than I did.

I did yoga breathing all the way up the stairs to the second floor. It didn't help. By the time I got to the principal's office, I was shaking like a leaf. There was no one in the waiting room, just me and a row of empty turquoise chairs. I sat down in one and waited for five minutes. It was totally quiet in there. The only sound was the ticking of the wall clock.

After waiting a few more minutes, I decided that Principal Pfeiffer wasn't coming, so I got up and headed for the door. Just as I stepped into the hall, I saw Spencer walking out of the counselor's office. *Oh no,* I thought. *Please don't look this way.* I really truly deeply did not want him to see me waiting in the principal's office. I ducked quickly back into the waiting room, but it was too late. He had spotted me.

"Hey, you," he said, sticking his face inside the open door. "I was just thinking about you. Is everything okay?"

"Sure, why wouldn't it be okay?"

"Um, because you're in the principal's office?"

"Oh, yeah, that. I don't know what he wants. Probably just to talk to me about tennis. He's got a little kid who's learning to play."

"Well, he picked the right person to talk to," Spencer said.

The clock on the wall ticked again. I heard footsteps coming up the stairs, and I thought I heard Principal Pfeiffer's voice.

"Listen, Spencer, you better go before he gets

here," I said. "I don't know if Principal Pfeiffer wants everyone to know about his son."

"What? That he plays tennis?"

"Well, he's got a really weak backhand. It's embarrassing, even for a five-year-old."

I pushed him out the door and closed it. Poor Spencer, he looked confused. But I didn't care. I just needed him gone. Two seconds later, the door burst open and Principal Pfeiffer entered, charging in at full speed. Lagging a few feet behind him was a man in a straw hat. I didn't recognize him.

"Sorry I'm late," Principal Pfeiffer said. Then, turning to the man in the straw hat, he said, "Is that the girl, Luz?"

The man in the straw hat looked at me carefully. I realized it was one of the school gardeners. Could it be the one who was outside the building that day, trimming the hedges? I saw him, but I didn't think he had seen me. He didn't look up, at least not that I saw.

"I think so, Señor Pfeiffer," he said. "She was wearing tennis clothes."

"Wait here please, Luz," the principal said, pointing to the chairs in his waiting room. "And you," he said, looking at me, "please come with me."

I followed him into his office and watched as he closed the door behind him. I didn't like that. If he just wanted to congratulate me on my tennis, there would be no need to close the door.

"Sit down," he commanded, taking a seat behind

his big oak desk. "We have a serious matter to discuss."

My heart was in my throat. I knew what was coming. I hated myself for what I had done, for having it come to this horrible moment.

"Luz came to me and said he saw someone matching your description in the teachers' lounge last Friday," he began. "I'm sure you understand we have to investigate a serious claim such as this. Students have no business in the teachers' lounge."

I couldn't look at him. I focused my eyes on a palm tree out the window. I would have paid a million dollars to disappear right then and there.

"I've spoken to your teachers to see if they noticed anything unusual going on with you, Charlie," he went on. "Most had nothing to report, but Mr. Newhart did point out that you did unusually well on your history midterm. Your best grade ever, by far, he said."

"I studied hard for that test," I said quietly.

"Did you, Charlie?"

There was a knock on the closed door to his office. I couldn't see who it was through the frosted glass, but from the size, I could tell it was a kid. At least it wasn't my dad. Principal Pfeiffer got up and opened the door. It was Sammie, looking confused and worried.

"What's going on?" she asked.

Luz had stood up and was staring at her like he'd seen a ghost.

"Maybe that's the one I saw," he said to Principal

Pfeiffer. "These girls, they look so much alike."

Sammie looked at me with panic in her eyes. She didn't have a clue why she was there.

"Were you wearing tennis clothes during sixth period last Friday?" Principal Pfeiffer barked at her.

"I don't know."

"You'd best know, young lady," he said, giving her an icy stare.

"Friday ... Friday ... yes ... Charlie and I played in the exhibition match that day. We changed at lunch. But what difference does that make? What's going on here?"

"That will be all, Luz," Principal Pfeiffer said to him. "You may go. And thank you for your honesty. You did the right thing."

Sammie looked really terrified now. She searched my eyes to get some sign of what this was all about. Principal Pfeiffer didn't give her much time to wonder.

"It appears that one of you snuck into the teachers' lounge last Friday," he said. "And it appears that one of you may have removed a test. A test, I might add, that your sister seemed to do unusually well on."

"You think I stole a test?" Sammie said. She was yelling. "That's the craziest thing I ever heard."

"Is it, Sammie? I don't think so. Mr. Newhart has pointed out that he keeps the test copies in a file cabinet in the teachers' lounge. The one where Luz believes he saw you."

Sammie jumped to her feet like she was going to haul off and slug him.

"Let me tell you something, Principal Pfeiffer. We don't steal. You can ask my sister. She'll tell you."

They both turned to look at me. I opened my mouth to talk but nothing came out. Just a raspy whisper that sounded like I was choking. I was choking. I was choking on the truth.

"There is a great writer named William Shakespeare," Principal Pfeiffer said. "Have you ever heard of him, Sammie?"

"Of course I have. I'm not stupid."

"Well, Shakespeare once wrote a play called *Hamlet*, and in it he wrote, 'The lady doth protest too much, methinks.'"

"What's that supposed to mean?" Sammie snarled.

"It means that sometimes the person who objects the loudest is actually the person who's guilty of the crime."

Every part of my body wanted to jump up and tell him to lay off Sammie. She was innocent. She had nothing to do with this. But it was as if some kind of paralysis had come over me. My feet and arms were heavy. My head was throbbing. My mouth was dry. All I could do, and I mean this, was sit there and stare at the palm tree out the window. Maybe you've heard the phrase "frozen with fear." That's what I was. Literally frozen with fear.

Principal Pfeiffer reached into his pocket and

pulled out a crumpled piece of paper. He put it on the edge of his desk.

"Does this look familiar to either of you?" he asked.

It was the note written in green ink that the General had passed to me just before I left Mr. Newhart's class. The one that said, *You're next.* with an arrow at the top.

I could feel all the blood literally drain from my face.

"I've never seen it before in my life," Sammie said.

"It was found in Mr. Newhart's file drawer. He doesn't recognize it as being his handwriting."

Principal Pfeiffer looked over at me. I shook my head. There was no way I could confess to knowing what it was. Then the General would be involved. I couldn't do that. I had promised not to tell. Even GoGo had said that a promise between friends was a sacred promise. Principal Pfeiffer sighed.

"I'm going to dismiss you two girls and give you some time to consider the accusation," Principal Pfeiffer told us. "I'm going to call a special meeting of the Honor Board for tomorrow morning. I'll expect you both in the counseling conference room at eight thirty. You'll have a chance to explain yourselves to your fellow students. The ultimate decision will be theirs."

"Fine," Sammie said. "They'll have nothing to say, because we're innocent."

Without even glancing at me, she got up and stomped out. Principal Pfeiffer looked at me long and hard.

"A lie weaves a tangled web," he said, his eyes practically boring a hole in me. "I strongly suggest you girls untangle yourselves and tell the truth."

With that, he picked up the General's crumpled note, put it back in his pocket, and marched out, leaving me alone in the office, staring at that same stupid palm tree.

Sister Trouble

....

Chapter 10

"We have to talk," Sammie said. "Immediately."

She was waiting for me in the hall as I staggered out of Principal Pfeiffer's office. She was crying but without tears, the kind of crying you do when you're too mad to actually weep.

"We can't talk here," I told her. "We have to find someplace private."

"Fine. How about if we go into the teachers' lounge? You seem to know how to get in there."

"Sammie, you have to give me a chance to explain."

"Oh, just like Principal Pfeiffer gave me a chance to explain? I was guilty before I even opened my mouth. How could you put me in that position?"

Ms. King stuck her head out of the counselor's office and held her finger up to her lips.

"*Shhhh,* girls. Can you please keep it down out here? We're administering some tests inside and it's very distracting."

"We have to get out of here. Let's go outside on the grass," I suggested.

"Great. And let's be sure to say hello to the gardener while we're out there. Maybe you can point out to him that I'm not you, that we're two different people. For one, I weigh twenty pounds more than you. Oh, sorry, fifteen, I lost five pounds. And what's the other thing? Oh yeah, I don't take things that don't belong to me and then lie about it."

She didn't shut up all the way down the stairs. She just kept hammering me about what a lousy, rotten, horrible person I am. At that moment, I couldn't have agreed with her more. It wasn't until we reached the patch of grass outside the main building that she shut up. I plopped down in a pathetic heap and just held my head in my hands. Sammie grew quiet, but her silence was worse than the talking.

"I assume it was you who walked off with the test," she said at last, "because I know it wasn't me. Why did you do it? Was getting an A so important?"

"I didn't cheat on the test, Sammie. I swear to you."

"But you stole it from the teachers' lounge, right? It was really you the gardener saw."

I didn't answer, but I didn't have to. My face said it all.

"Charlie, I don't understand. If you didn't do it for a grade, then why? Why'd you take it? For fun?"

I shook my head. Suddenly, Sammie's confused expression changed, and I saw the realization hit her—that I hadn't done it for me, but for someone else. She threw her backpack on the ground and sat down next to me.

"You gave it to Lauren," she said, her voice boiling over with anger. "You did it for her, didn't you?"

Again I didn't answer, but she had come to the truth on her own.

"I can't believe it," she yelled at me. "What kind of friend asks another friend to do something like that? To steal and cheat for them?"

"Lauren didn't ask me to."

"Then who did?"

"I can't say."

I could see Sammie biting her lower lip furiously. She had that look on her face, the one she gets when she's frowning really hard. Her forehead squinches up in big worry lines and the freckle above her eyebrow drops down closer to her nose. I do the same thing, but my freckle is over my left eyebrow, and hers is over the right one. GoGo always says that when we were babies, it was the only way she could tell us apart.

"Any one of them could have put you up to this," she muttered. "Or all of them. Those Sporty Forty kids stick together like glue."

"They're my friends, Sammie. You'd do the same for your friends. You'd help them if they were in trouble."

"No one was in trouble, Charlotte."

"Lauren was, Samantha."

"Oh really? Why? Because she wasn't going to get to go to some party? Because she'd have to stay in and study for a change? Because for the first time in her spoiled little life her daddy wasn't going to give her everything she wanted? I can't believe you fell for that. I didn't think you were that stupid."

I burst into tears. It was as if the full realization of what I'd done flew up and hit me in the face. I didn't know what to do next. My one true best friend, my sister, was losing respect for me by the minute. I sobbed and sobbed and sobbed.

"Lauren is not your friend," Sammie said to me in a kinder voice. "She's two-faced. She uses you to get what she wants—to get close to Ryan or to get something else she wants, like that test. Then she talks about you behind your back."

"Excuse me," said a voice from behind us. "But if we are talking about being two-faced, I'd say that's what you're being right now, Miss Sammie I'm-Better-Than-Everyone Diamond."

We both looked up to see Lauren standing there with her hands on her hips. In the midst of all the emotion, neither of us had realized the bell had rung and students were starting to leave class and circulate on the school grounds.

Sammie stiffened as Lauren took a seat next to us.

"Charlie," she said, offering me one of her strawberry-scented tissues. "I am so sorry. I went to the principal's office as soon as science was over. I figured out what happened, and I want you to know I'm here for you."

Sammie rolled her eyes. "You shouldn't have asked her to do it in the first place."

"I didn't. And as for you, Sammie, you don't know what you're talking about. Charlie is my friend. She is one of us. I am not two-faced, and in the future, I'd prefer it if you didn't talk behind my back."

"In the future, I'd prefer it if you didn't use my sister as your doormat."

"Cut it out, Sammie," I said. "This isn't helping."

What was also not helping was the crowd of students piling out of the building and making their way to their classes. I felt totally conspicuous, all teary-eyed and miserable-looking. I'm sure everyone was staring at me, wondering what awful thing had happened to me.

"Hey, you guys," Alicia yelled from across the lawn.

"Can't you keep her away?" Lauren said to Sammie. "We have personal business to discuss here."

But Alicia was already halfway across the lawn, running up to where we were sitting.

"Where've you been, Sam-I-Am?" she said cheerfully. "Somebody said you had to go see the principal. What's up with that?"

When Sammie didn't answer, Alicia looked over at my tear-streaked face and red-rimmed eyes and running nose and immediately took in the situation.

"Uh-oh," she said. "Looks like I've arrived at a bad time."

"Actually, Alicia, you got here just at the right time," Sammie told her. "Charlie has gotten herself into a little trouble, but luckily Lauren is here for her. Aren't you, Lauren?"

"I'm sure Charlie and I can fix this," Lauren said. "And yes, I am here for her."

"The bell's going to ring," Sammie said, standing up and throwing her backpack over her shoulder. "I have to go. Alicia, I'll see you after school at the Truth Tellers meeting. I could use a little shot of truth."

"Look, I don't know what's happening here," Alicia said to Sammie, "but I'm sure it's fine if you skip the meeting today. I'll tell Ms. Carew you're busy with family matters."

"You can go to your little drama-wama group," Lauren said. "Charlie and I have the situation totally under control."

To my surprise, Sammie headed off with Alicia. The only thing she said to me as she left was, "You've got to do the right thing, Charles. Just do the right thing."

I felt sick to my stomach. Lauren watched them go, then stood up and helped me up, too.

"We're supposed to go to cheerleading practice after school," she said, "but maybe we should skip it. We can go to Starbucks and talk this out. It's amazing what a good Frappuccino can fix."

"I don't want to go to Starbucks, Lauren."

"Right, too many people there. Okay, then let's get some water now. Water will help, and I don't care if I'm late to class. I would do anything for you."

We walked down the gravel path to the water fountain by the art building. It was off the main drag and not many kids were there, just one or two who were unloading the ceramics kiln. I noticed that one of them was Will Lee, the little sixth-grader who'd been trailing around after Alicia and Sammie. He waved, much too enthusiastically as far as I was concerned, but I didn't wave back. I stuck my face in the fountain and let water splash all over it. Then I took the longest drink in the history of the world. After I had downed probably fifty buckets of water, I felt well enough to tell Lauren what had happened in Principal Pfeiffer's office, every horrible detail.

"This isn't as bad as you think," she said when I had poured out the whole story. "My dad's a lawyer, and the one thing he always says is that you have to have evidence to convict someone. And they don't have any evidence that you or Sammie took the test or took anything for that matter."

I leaned against the brick wall of the art building. Will Lee waved again, and I ignored him again.

"But what about the gardener?" I asked. "He says he saw me."

"You just said he couldn't even say if it was you or Sammie he saw, so how much is his opinion worth, anyway? It could have been any girl on the tennis team. You all mostly look alike. I say you just deny everything. They can't prove a thing. Besides, it's not a crime to go into the teachers' lounge. Tons of people go in there without swiping a test."

I considered everything she said. I thought it made sense, but I couldn't really tell. My head was spinning, and I felt dizzy. I had always thought I knew right from wrong, but now the line between the two seemed so blurry. I leaned my head against the warm bricks and sighed.

"Hey, Charles, I do have one question," Lauren said after a minute. "You didn't tell Principal Pfeiffer about me, did you? You know, that you gave the test to me."

"No, Lauren. I wouldn't do that. I promised I wouldn't tell. And a promise between friends is sacred."

She leaned over and gave me a big hug.

"I knew I could always count on you," she whispered. "Now should we get to class?"

"You go on," I said. "I need to be alone for a while. To think things through."

"Okay. But really, Charlie, don't worry so much

about it. No one ever has to know what really happened. And besides, we have a lot of friends on the Honor Board. They'll be on your side. I'll call later to check up on you."

After she left, I managed to pry myself away from the brick wall and make it over to a nearby ledge. I plopped down on that stupid little ledge and pointed my face up to the sun. The heat burned my cheeks, and I felt the muscles in my shoulders start to relax. My body went limp. I closed my eyes and lay there completely still, like a large reptile basking in the sun. I didn't want to think about anything. I just wanted to go back to the way it was, before my dad lost his job, before my mom left, before we lived at the Sporty Forty, when Sammie and I were just two regular little sixth-graders at Culver City Middle School. Things were so much easier then.

"You look like a lizard," someone said to me. "Did you know that lizards smell with their tongues?"

When I opened my eyes, I saw that it was Will Lee talking to me.

"Not now, Will. I'm not in the mood for weird lizard facts."

"How about weird gecko facts, then? Geckos are actually a subset of the lizard family. Did you know they're the only lizards that can vocalize?"

"Can you please go away now?"

"Are you sick? Do you feel bad? Do you need help?"

"No, yes, and yes."

"So you're not sick, but you do feel bad, and you do need help." He scratched his head. "Sounds like you're having a bad day, emotionally speaking."

I opened my eyes and stared at him. What sixth-grade boy talks like that?

"How old are you?" I asked him.

"Ten. I skipped third grade."

"So tell me, Will, how'd you get to be so smart, emotionally speaking, if you're only ten?"

"From Truth Tellers. I listen to everybody. We tell the truth about our lives. Your sister, Sammie, is really good at it. You probably are, too."

"Apparently, I stink at telling the truth."

"Is that why you're feeling bad right now?"

"If you must know, Will, I did something bad to protect a friend. But I promised I'd never tell anyone else about it. And now my lie has grown really big and involved someone I care about. And that's why I'm feeling bad. Because I can't tell the truth, and I can't keep up the lie. I'm stuck. Trapped."

"Like a lizard that's been caught." He nodded. "Except if they get caught and lose their tails, they can grow new ones. Of course, the new one is shorter than the old one and doesn't have any bones."

"Will, I thought we went over this. No weird lizard facts."

"Sorry."

"Not your fault. I'm the one who got myself into

this mess. And I don't know the right way to fix it. I don't know what's right and what's wrong anymore."

What was I doing, talking to this very short ten-year-old about my emotional dilemma? I wanted to stop, but I couldn't. It felt really good to be talking to him.

"I'm going to Truth Tellers after school," he said. "Ms. Carew called a special meeting today. You should come. It might make you feel better."

"I'm not part of your group, Will."

"Anyone can be a Truth Teller," he answered. "All you have to do is express your true self and listen with your heart. Ms. Carew says those are the only rules. Oh, and you have to be kind."

"Well, that leaves me out," I said with a laugh. "I'm a nasty, hateful person."

He scratched his head again. "You seem nice to me. Anyway, if you want to come, we're in Ms. Carew's room. By the way, I think you're very attractive."

And then he walked off toward the main building. As I watched him go, I couldn't believe how my opinion of him had changed from just that short conversation. Two minutes ago, I thought he was an annoying kid with too many lizard facts. Then we talked, with no games and no lies and no trying to be anything other than what we were. Him, a slightly weird ten-year-old. Me, a very sad person who had disappointed herself. And look what happened. I had grown to like the kid, even though he was pretty much a weirdo.

Maybe there really was something to this Truth Tellers group. Maybe if I went, I could find a way to talk to Sammie, to make her hear me. If I expressed my true self, maybe she could listen with her heart and forgive me. It was worth a try.

I really can't tell you what happened the rest of the day. It was a total blur. I spent a lot of time in the girls' bathroom. I sat in class but didn't hear a word. I went to the library during lunch and stared at an open book without reading one word. Mostly, I waited for after school to come, hoping that going to Truth Tellers would help me get rid of that horrible knot in my stomach.

After seventh period, I headed toward Ms. Carew's room, which was on the first floor, in a room they call the Patio Room because it has a small balcony surrounded by trees and bushes. Sammie had told me that sometimes Truth Tellers met out there.

I walked quietly down the hall, not wanting my footsteps to disturb the meeting. As I approached Ms. Carew's room, I heard voices coming from inside. I heard Sammie's voice and others, too. I couldn't hear what they were saying, but it sounded intense.

I poked my head inside the door and looked around. I was totally unprepared for what I saw.

Truth Tellers

....

Chapter 11

"You can do it," a girl with bright green streaks in her hair was saying to Sammie. "Just imagine how good you'll feel when the truth is out."

Sammie was standing in the middle of a circle of kids who were seated around her. She was talking and crying at the same time—real tears this time, the kind that run down your face and into the corners of your mouth. The girl with the green hair was next to her, one arm around her shoulders for support, although how much support someone wearing black fingernail polish can provide is beyond me. Ms. Carew was part of the circle, as were Alicia and Sara and Will Lee and about nine other kids I didn't know.

"She didn't even care that I could get expelled for this," Sammie burst out, crying as she talked. "Imagine how it feels—my own sister doing the most selfish, mean thing anyone has ever done to me."

I stood there in the hall, feeling like someone had punched me in the stomach. I knew she felt that way, but it seemed like such a betrayal to be telling everyone about the incident. These weird kids who didn't even know me.

"Sometimes people we love disappoint us," Ms. Carew said to Sammie. "And because we love them, it hurts all the more."

A couple of the kids nodded.

"My sister always calls me metal mouth," a girl with braces chimed in. "Especially when I have friends over because she's jealous that I'm not playing with her."

"My sister tells me I'm stupid," Will said, "because I like art better than math. I know I'm not a brainiac like her, but it makes me mad when she points it out."

"You're very smart, Will," Sara said. "And you make beautiful stuff in ceramics. She probably just wishes she was as multitalented as you."

"Relationships with brothers and sisters are very complex," Ms. Carew said. "They require a lot of mutual understanding."

"Well, there's no way I'm going to understand what my sister has done," Sammie said. "She's gotten me in big trouble, and for what? To protect Lauren Wadsworth, who wouldn't know how to be a real friend if she tried."

What???? I couldn't believe my ears! She actually said Lauren's name. That was *my* secret, *my* sworn secret. I had promised *never* to reveal what happened, and here was Sammie, just blabbing it out to the whole world. A surge of anger rose up inside me like a tidal wave.

"You can't do that!" I found myself screaming from the hall.

Everyone in the circle turned around and stared at me. Sammie seemed surprised but not sorry.

"This is Truth Tellers," she said. "Unlike yourself, we don't tell lies in here."

"This is none of your business, Sammie. And certainly none of theirs."

Ms. Carew got up from the circle, came over to me, and reached out her hand.

"Would you like to come in and join us, Charlie? I think it might help."

"I promised not to talk about this, Ms. Carew," I answered. "And Sammie has no right, no right at all to blab about this. If she wants to tell the stupid truth, let her tell it about her own life, not mine."

"Come in," Ms. Carew insisted, taking me by the hand. I wanted to resist but I found myself following her like a little puppy. She was wearing a beautiful, colorful top made of African fabric, and she smelled sweet, like an orange mango smoothie. Her hand was soft yet strong. The minute she touched me, I became aware of an overwhelming feeling of exhaustion. I was more tired than I had ever been in my life. I just wanted this all to be over so I could rest.

As I walked into the room, I was surprised by a chorus of voices welcoming me.

"Hey, Charlie, welcome to Truth Tellers," Alicia said.

"You're in a safe place," Sara added.

"There's no judgment here," the girl with the braces said.

"Sit down in the circle, Charlie," Ms. Carew said.

"No, thanks, I'll stand."

"It's important that you sit so you can join our acceptance circle," Ms. Carew said. "When you join the circle, you agree that each person here is accepted for exactly who they are. And what we say here stays here. Right, kids?"

"Our lips are sealed," Will said, pretending to zip his lips together. He was so mature in so many ways that it was odd to see him doing such a babyish gesture. Everyone else pretended to zip their lips, too, even the girl with the green hair and black fingernails.

"I'm Etta," she said. "And you can trust me."

"Etta, why don't you sit back down in the circle," Ms. Carew said. "Charlie, please join us. And Sammie, come sit next to your sister."

"I'd rather sit next to Alicia," Sammie said.

"I know you're hurt, but it's important that you and Charlie have the courage to talk this out honestly,"

Ms. Carew said. "You're going to look at each other and tell the truth."

Sammie sat down cross-legged next to me, but stuffed her sweatshirt in between us so there was no possibility of our legs touching. I recognized that gesture. She used to do it all the time when we were losing a tennis match. Our dad made us talk to each other during breaks to make sure we were communicating. She would always stuff her warm-up suit between us on the bench. I used to think it was because she didn't want her sweaty leg touching mine, but now I realized it was a way to put up a little wall to protect herself in case I said something critical like "You should come to the net more often" or "You've got to get your second serve in." She hates being criticized. Come to think of it, so do I.

"How are you feeling, Sammie?" Ms. Carew asked.

"Angry. Disappointed. Scared."

I nodded. I was feeling all the same things.

"Charlie," Ms. Carew said, turning to me. "Sammie has told us how she feels about what you've done. I'm sure you have many feelings, too. You secret is safe with us. It's important to tell your sister why you did it. Dig deep, Charlie, and tell the truth."

"I don't know why I did it," I said. "I just did."

"Did you think you were doing something wrong at the time?" Alicia asked.

"I guess. At first, anyway. But then everyone told

me how great it was to help . . ." I paused, reluctant to say her name.

"Lauren," Sammie said with a snarky tone in her voice.

"Right, to help her get through a rough time."

Sara Berlin, the girl with the poofy hair, spoke up. I thought everyone there would hate me for putting Sammie in this position. They were her friends. But Sara was surprisingly understanding.

"Those kids are a tough group to be accepted by," she said. "I can see why you'd agree to do something stupid to become part of them."

My first reaction was to deny what she said. I didn't think I wanted to be a part of the SF2s that desperately that I'd do anything to be accepted. But someone else spoke up before I had time to object. It was Alicia.

"When I first came to America," she said, "I was so afraid of all the kids around me. I didn't look like them, I didn't speak their language, and they all seemed so rich. Back home in El Salvador, we didn't ride in fancy cars or wear different clothes to school every day. I felt like such an outsider."

An outsider. That was an interesting word to use. It's the way Sammie and I felt just a month ago when we arrived at the Sporty Forty and transferred to Beachside. We spoke the same language as everyone else, but we weren't like them. Funny, just like Alicia, those kids seemed rich and rode in fancy cars and wore different clothes to school every day. I wanted to be one of them. I still did.

"No one wants to be an outsider," I heard myself agreeing.

"It's easy to make bad decisions to be part of a group," an overweight kid named Devon said. "When I joined the baseball team, everyone shaved their heads as a show of team spirit. I did it, too, but some people are just not meant to shave their heads. I had to walk around looking like a big walnut head for two months."

The kids all laughed. And to my surprise, I found myself smiling, too.

"Looking back on it now," Etta said to me. "Do you think that's why you took the test? To be accepted by the group?"

"I'm sure that was part of it," I said, hating to admit the truth, but knowing I had to. "But also, I really thought I was helping out my best friend."

"That's where you're wrong," Sammie said. "She's not your best friend."

"How do you know that?" I asked her. "I like Lauren. She's sweet to me. And she likes me. Why are you always on her case?"

Sammie didn't answer.

"Sammie?" Ms. Carew answered. "Your sister asked you a question. She deserves an honest answer."

"I'm entitled not to like her," Sammie said. "It's a free country."

"There has to be a reason you don't like her," Will said. "I think she's a very attractive girl." Everyone laughed, even Will. "What's wrong with that?"

"You're ten, dude," Sara said to him.

"Sammie, we're waiting for an answer," Ms. Carew said when the laughter had died down. I saw that freckle on Sammie's forehead moving down toward her nose. Obviously, she didn't like what she was thinking.

"It takes courage to tell the truth," Etta said to her. "Lay it on us, sister."

"Lauren's just so pretty," Sammie said finally. Her voice sounded like the words were stuck in her throat and didn't want to come out. "She's always perfect. Every time I'm around her, I feel fat."

"I can relate," Devon said. "Feeling fat sucks."

"That's an honest and brave statement you made, Sammie," Ms. Carew said. "Is that all you feel about Lauren?"

"Well, there is one other thing, but I don't know if it's important."

"All our feelings are important."

Sammie seemed to be struggling with what she wanted to say. "I feel kind of . . . sort of . . . I hate to admit it . . . but okay, here it is . . . I'm jealous of her."

"Because she's so attractive?" Will asked.

"You're not helping, Will," Alicia said. "Let her talk."

Sammie took a deep breath and looked up at me. There were tears in her eyes.

"Mostly, I'm jealous because she's your best friend.

And I always thought I was your best friend."

The tears were out of her eyes now, rolling down her face. She didn't sound angry anymore, just sad.

"That's how I felt when you became best friends with Alicia," I said. "I was hurt and jealous and confused. I couldn't understand why you'd pick her over me and my friends."

And then there were tears in my eyes, too, and on my face.

"We've always been so identical," she said. "And now we're different. I miss the old way."

"People grow up and become themselves," Ms. Carew said. "But that doesn't mean you have to lose each other. You just have to accept each other for who you are and respect your differences."

"Yeah," Will piped up. "That's why we're sitting in this acceptance circle."

I looked at Sammie sitting here with all her new friends. They weren't like my new friends, that's for sure. But they were nice and kind, and they cared about her. They even cared about me.

"I love you, Sammie," I said. "Nothing will ever change that."

"I love you, too, Charlie. I just don't love what you did."

"I'm so sorry I hurt you," I said, reaching for her and pulling that stupid sweatshirt out from between us.

"You got carried away with your new friends,

Charlie. I hope you see what they got you into."

"I'm going to make it right. You'll see."

"I hope so," she said, throwing her arms around my neck.

Before I knew it, all the other Truth Tellers had left the acceptance circle and formed a tight little one around us. It was a pretty classic group hug. I looked through my tears at the smiling faces of Etta and Devon and Will and Sara and Alicia—kids I had barely known until a few minutes before. And now I felt a real connection to them.

"It's amazing what telling the truth can do," Ms. Carew said as she watched everyone cluster around Sammie and me.

And I think there were a few tears in her eyes, too.

The Honor Board

....

Chapter 12

"On behalf of the student body of Beachside Middle School, and as the selected chairperson of our committee, I hereby call this special meeting of the Honor Board to order," Phoebe Lee said, pounding the small wooden gavel down on the table.

It was the next morning, and the clock on the wall of the counselor's conference room said 8:32. Sammie and I were sitting on one side of a long, shiny oak meeting table. Ms. King was at one end and Principal Pfeiffer was at the other. In front of him on the table, he had a yellow pad and a pen, ready to write down every terrible thing about me. Resting on the pad was the crumpled-up note with the green arrow that the General had written to me. Each time the big hand on the clock ticked forward, Principal Pfeiffer looked at his watch impatiently and smoothed his hair with his fingers, which was not actually necessary since he was bald. It must have been a nervous habit left over from when he had hair.

Across from us, seated in brown leather chairs, were the members of the Honor Board. When Sammie and I started at Beachside, we had to attend an orientation that explains the Honor Code at our school. It says that every student is expected to practice honesty in all academic and social endeavors. Any violations are brought before the Honor Board, which consists of five student representatives selected by the faculty.

One of the brown chairs was empty, which meant only four Honor Board members were present. I wondered who was missing.

"It is the responsibility of the Honor Board to hear specific cases in which the school's Honor System may have been violated," Phoebe was saying. "The board has been asked by Principal Pfeiffer to hear the case of Samantha and Charlotte Diamond. Principal Pfeiffer, would you like to begin?"

"You go ahead, Phoebe," he said. "I'm going to let the board handle this. The Honor System belongs to the students. We trust that your ruling will be fair."

He ran his fingers over his bald head and picked up his pen. He started tapping it on the yellow pad without even looking down, so his pen made a cluster of random little ink marks here and there. I had a feeling Principal Pfeiffer had filled a lot of yellow sheets of paper with those random dots. No one else seemed to notice, but to me, each little tap of his pen sounded like a mini explosion. I was going to have to concentrate on putting that sound out of my head.

"Okay," Phoebe said. "We'll begin. The members of the board will introduce themselves to Sammie and Charlie. I'm Phoebe Lee, seventh-grade representative and chairperson."

"I'm Lily March, also representing the seventh grade."

I had been surprised to see Lily sitting there when I came in. She had never mentioned to me that she was on the Honor Board, but I think kids who are on it aren't really supposed to talk about it. She's probably who Lauren was referring to when she said we had friends on the Honor Board. When Sammie and I were first ushered in, Lily didn't look at me, and I could tell she was having trouble now. I couldn't blame her, I was embarrassed, too. You don't want to ever be in a position where you have to judge a friend.

"I'm Justin Hawkins, representing the eighth grade."

Justin was a tall guy who I recognized as being one of Ryan's buddies from the volleyball team. I didn't know much about him, only that he was a straight-A student, and the guys on the team called him Bounce.

"I'm Olivia Feldman, representing the eighth grade."

I didn't know her, but figured she must be Ben's older sister. Funny, it was her brother's invitation that started all this, and now here she was to decide my fate. I'm sure she could never have known how much trouble her family's party had made for me. Okay, you're right. I made the trouble for myself, but my point was, it all started with Ben's invitation. Olivia wore glasses like Ben's and was wearing a fringed leather top that I had seen in the window of my favorite store on the Third Street Promenade. I remember looking at it and wondering who had the money to buy such an expensive thing. Now I knew. I had never seen Olivia at the Sporty Forty, so I guessed that even though her parents could afford to be members, she wasn't the beach type.

Phoebe looked up at the clock. It was 8:36. I prayed that this hearing would start soon. I was so nervous I felt like there was an egg beater inside my stomach. Sammie looked pale and scared. Neither of us had slept all night. GoGo kept trying to get us to play Scrabble with her, but we told her that we were exhausted and needed to go to bed early. Luckily, our dad wasn't there to poke his nose into things. GoGo said he'd been called up to the Santa Barbara Racquet Club to substitute for an official that got food poisoning and had to stay overnight. Ryan had been acting weird all evening, telling lame knock-knock jokes in his Kermit voice, but I didn't think it was because he knew anything was up with us. I think he just acts weird to amuse himself.

"Should we begin, Principal Pfeiffer?" Phoebe asked. "One of our members doesn't seem to be showing up, and I don't know how long you ..."

Before she could finish the sentence, the door to the counseling office burst open. It was the fifth member of the Honor Board, full of apologies for being late. I knew that voice. I closed my eyes and wished on everything I had ever wished on. Shooting stars. Rainbows. Birthday candles. Dandelions. A fallen eyelash.

Please, I wished. *Please don't let that be who I think it is. Please. Please.*

But wishes don't always come true, and in this case, mine didn't. It was Spencer Ballard, he of the great abs and adorable dimple, apologizing like crazy for being late.

"Sorry, folks. My dad couldn't find the clicker for the garage door, and it turned out that our dog had hidden it in ..."

He stopped mid-sentence when he saw Sammie and me. To say he was surprised would be the understatement of the year. His mouth dropped open, and his eyes furrowed so deep it looked like he had a unibrow.

"What are you doing here?" he asked.

I couldn't look at him. I put my hands to my face and covered my eyes.

"Sammie and Charlie have been accused of violating the Honor Code," Phoebe said. "They're here to tell us their side of the story."

Spencer looked really confused as he took his place in one of the brown chairs.

"Charlie?" he said softly. "Is that true?"

I wanted to run as far away as possible. To Outer Mongolia. Or Timbuktu. I don't even know where those places are, but they sounded like they were the right distance from Beachside Middle School.

Phoebe cleared her throat.

"Here are the facts of the case," she said, sounding a little too much like a TV lawyer for my taste. "The gardener, Luz Enriquez, reported to the principal that he saw someone matching your descriptions, dressed in a tennis outfit, entering the teachers' lounge last Friday. Principal Pfeiffer has reason to suspect one of you went in there and took a copy of Mr. Newhart's history exam for the purpose of cheating. How do you answer these accusations?"

I could see Sammie's hands shaking in her lap. I had told her not to worry, that I would do the right thing, but she seemed like she was going to cry at any minute. It was the most nerve-wracking thing either of us had ever faced—much worse than the tiebreaker at the all-state tennis finals, which was off the charts on the stress scale. We both knew that our very existence at Beachside was at stake. In twenty minutes, we could be expelled.

"I'd like to speak first," I said. I didn't look at Spencer, but I could tell his eyes were focused on me. Instead, I looked right into Bounce's eyes. He was the most neutral person there. I tried to ignore the tap-tap-tapping of Principal Pfeiffer's pen and focus on what I had planned to say. It wasn't easy.

"I'd like to request that you let my sister leave this hearing right now," I began. "She had nothing to do with this. I was the one who went into the teachers' lounge. I was the one the gardener saw. Sammie did nothing wrong. She just has the bad luck to look exactly like me."

"That's not such bad luck, if you ask me," Bounce said.

"This isn't a joking matter, Mr. Hawkins," Principal Pfeiffer said.

"Sorry," he said. "I was just trying to lighten things up."

Principal Pfeiffer put down his pen and shook his head.

"Inappropriate," was all he said. "Ms. Diamond, go on."

"This whole incident has caused my sister a lot of pain," I continued. "She is the last person in the world that I would ever want to hurt. So I apologize to her in front of all of you and ask that you let her go on to class."

"Does anyone want to ask Sammie anything?" Phoebe asked the group.

"If she wasn't there, then there's no reason to," Olivia said.

Lily, who has been nervously twisting her finger around her curly black hair, spoke up. "Madam Chairperson, I think we should take a vote."

"All in favor of dismissing any accusations against Sammie Diamond, raise your hand," Phoebe said.

All five hands went up in the air. Actually, six hands went up in the air, because Ms. King voted, too. I saw Principal Pfeiffer whisper to her that the adults were nonvoting members of the board, and she put her hand down. I could tell she wanted to vote, though. Everyone says she's a big fan of the students and always on our side.

Phoebe picked up the wooden gavel and banged it on the table.

"It's unanimous," she said. "Sammie, the board has cleared you of any accusations. You may go to class."

"I'd like to stay here, if it's okay with you guys," she said in a shaky voice. "To support my sister."

"I think that's a lovely thing to do, Sammie." Ms. King nodded.

I wanted Sammie to stay for selfish reasons, so I'd have a friendly face to look to for the rest of the hearing. But for her sake, I wanted her to go. She had been through enough because of me and what was about to follow wasn't going to be pleasant.

"I'm okay, Sams," I whispered to her. "Really. You can go."

"I'm staying, Charlie. End of discussion."

Principal Pfeiffer was dotting up a storm on his yellow pad. You could just tell that he was bursting with things to say and it was hard for him to let the students run the meeting. He had a little breakdown and temporarily took charge.

"Ms. Diamond," he said. "I believe you owe the board an explanation of what you were doing in the teachers' lounge. Your behavior in there is at the heart of this serious matter."

I saw Spencer move up to the edge of his chair. The moment was here, the question I had to face. How was I going to say this? What would Spencer think of me afterward? He already looked so sad and disappointed. I tried to speak, but the words didn't come and I sat there for a long minute. My mind wandered to a far-off time, when Sammie and I were four years old, and we had run behind the counter in King Pin Doughnut Shop. When our mom wasn't looking, we lifted two doughnut holes from the tray and popped them into our mouths. We couldn't even lie about having stolen them, because the chocolate sprinkles were all over our lips.

"I'm so disappointed in you girls," our mom had said. "You know better than to steal."

We promised we'd never do it again.

Sammie's voice brought me back to the reality of the hearing.

"Just tell the truth, Charlie," she whispered to me. "I know it's hard, but it won't be once you get started. Ms. Carew always says the truth will set you free."

All eyes in the room were on me. It was silent except for the persistent tapping of Principal Pfeiffer's pen. Everyone was waiting. I had no choice. I was trapped. So I took a deep breath and plunged in. The truth came out in one big uncontrollable gush.

"I went into the teachers' lounge because I knew that a copy of our history test was in Mr. Newhart's file cabinet. When no one was looking, I opened the file cabinet and took a copy of the test. I stole it."

Olivia gasped. Bounce's eyebrows shot up in surprise. Phoebe shook her head disapprovingly. Ms. King covered her eyes with her hand. And Lily's chin trembled like she was holding back tears. I couldn't bear to look at Spencer.

"You didn't really do that," he said softly.

Then I looked at him, square in the eye.

"Yes, I did."

A hush fell over the room. Lily and Spencer looked so sad and uncomfortable. Olivia looked shocked. Phoebe just continued to shake her head disapprovingly. At last, Bounce spoke up.

"So what you're telling us is that you looked up the answers and cheated on the midterm?" he said.

"No, I didn't. I was wrong to steal the test. Very

wrong. And I am so sorry that I did. But I did not look at it. The good grade that I got on that midterm was because I studied. It was all my work. I swear that to you."

"I remember you studying last weekend," Spencer said. "You had your book at the tournament. And you told me your grandma was quizzing you."

"I stole, but I didn't cheat," I repeated. "I know that sounds weird, but it's the truth."

"So why'd you do it?" Olivia asked. "Why'd you take the test?"

That was the really hard question, the one I'd been dreading. I closed my eyes and tried to be brave. I reached inside myself and pulled up every ounce of courage I had. And I remembered GoGo's words. A promise between friends is sacred. Whatever else I was, I was not a two-faced friend. I would keep my promise. When I opened my mouth to answer, I was surprised at how strong my voice sounded.

"I did it for a friend," I said. "But I swore that I would never reveal any more than that. If you want to ask me any further questions about that part of it, I'm afraid I can't answer them."

"Ms. Diamond," Principal Pfeiffer said, tossing his pen down on the table. "This is outrageous."

"I'm sorry, Principal Pfeiffer. I don't mean to disrespect you. But if I broke a promise, I would disrespect myself."

He stood up in his place as if he were going to

do something, then sat back down. We all watched as he rubbed his gray goatee with his hand in great frustration. He had more hair on his chin than he did on his head. Finally, he spoke in a quiet, controlled voice.

"If you tell us who the other students involved are, Ms. Diamond, the Honor Board may see fit to lighten your punishment. You understand that you will have to pay for what you did."

"I made a promise, Principal Pfeiffer. And a promise between friends is sacred."

"That's all very well and good, Ms. Diamond," he said. "Very noble indeed. Nonetheless, I think you should reconsider your decision."

"I have considered it carefully, sir. More than you know."

"You're being foolish," he snapped, rising to his feet.

"She's being loyal," Ms. King said. "And true to her word." She put an arm on him and gently pulled him back into a sitting position. "That's a rare quality these days."

Principal Pfeiffer picked up his pen and began tapping on his yellow pad. He was definitely not happy with me. It was really tense in there. Sammie reached out and took my hand. I was so glad she was there. I know I've said before that people think twins have all the same emotions and that it's not true. But I can promise you this: At that moment, Sammie was feeling everything I was feeling. We were truly two halves of the same circle.

"Well, then, is that all you have to say for yourself?" Principal Pfeiffer said at last. "Do you want to leave us with any last words in your defense?"

I stood up. I'm not sure where I got the courage to do that, but something inside made me rise to my feet. I wanted to stand tall, chin out and shoulders back.

"What I would like to say to the Honor Board is that I am so sorry for what I did. It was wrong and I learned a huge lesson. Our grandmother has explained to me that we all make mistakes. She says that's what it means to be alive. But she also has taught me that the most important thing is that we learn from our mistakes. That's what it means to be human."

Principal Pfeiffer stopped tapping his pencil.

"I will have to live with whatever punishment the board hands out," I said. "I understand that. But I promise everyone here that I will never repeat the mistake I made. And I think you know, as you've seen today, I keep my promises."

The room was totally quiet. I looked into the face of each member of the Honor Board and for the life of me, I couldn't tell what they were thinking.

The Verdict

....

Chapter 13

"Before the board begins its deliberation, I want to remind you, Ms. Diamond, that what you have admitted is a serious offense," Principal Pfeiffer said.

After I sat down, the board had spent another ten minutes asking me questions about how I planned to learn from what I had done. Phoebe made a weak attempt to ask again who else was involved, but Lily spoke up and said that she thought they should respect my sacred pledge. She looked over to Spencer for support, but he didn't say anything. I noticed that he kept glancing at the crumpled note that was still sitting on the table in front of Principal Pfeiffer. I wondered if he recognized the General's green ink and distinctive handwriting. After all, they had grown up together. He had probably gotten hundreds of notes from him over the years. The note didn't attract Lily's attention, which made me pretty sure she didn't recognize the General's handwriting. But Spencer couldn't take his eyes off it.

After a while, Spencer saw me looking at him, and when our eyes met, I was sure that he knew the note was from the General. He didn't have to say a word, I could see it in his eyes. Now he was part of this, too. Was he going to have to tell the Honor Board? I had promised to keep the secret, but he hadn't. Without meaning to, I had made Spencer part of this horrible incident. I was beginning to realize what Principal Pfeiffer meant when he said that lies spin tangled webs.

"Okay, we're going to ask you to wait outside while we come to a verdict on your case," Phoebe said in a very businesslike and unfriendly manner. "We'll call you back in when we've reached our decision."

"Thank you all for listening," I said as Sammie and I got up and walked to the door. I was already wondering how on earth I was going to tell my dad that I had gotten expelled. He would be furious, and then he'd have to call my mom in Boston and she would say, "Oh, Charlie, I'm so disappointed in you. You know better than to steal."

Stupid me. I hadn't made any progress since I was four years old.

The only good thing about being out in the hall was that there was circulating air. Inside that room, it had gotten so hot and stuffy that I thought I was going to suffocate.

"Your neck has disappeared," Sammie said, putting her hands out and pushing down on my shoulders, which had crept up to my ears from all the stress. "You look like a turtle."

"I'd like to be a turtle right now. Then I could disappear into my shell and never come out."

"Yeah, but you'd be all wrinkly and ugly and walk really slow like this," Sammie said, making her eyes bulge out and doing a turtle-crawling gesture with her hands and feet. She was trying to lighten the mood. I let out a weak laugh, just to let her know how much I appreciated her attempt.

"Oh, thank goodness you're laughing." I whirled around to see Lauren running up the stairs. "Everything must have turned out okay."

She bounded over and threw her arms around me.

"How'd you get out of class?" I asked her.

"Are you kidding me? You think I could sit there while you're going through such agony? I told Mr. Weinstock that I had forgotten my homework in my locker, and he let me go."

"We're still waiting," I told her. "They're discussing their decision."

"Good, then there's still time," Lauren said. "I wanted to bring this to you."

She reached into the pocket of her salmon-colored cashmere sweater and pulled out a gold bracelet.

"It's my lucky charm bracelet," she said. "Wear it. I'll help you put it on."

"She can't wear that," Sammie said.

"Why not? It always brings me good luck. It's very special. Look at this charm. It's a calendar of August with a little ruby on the twenty-third, which is my birthday. And check out the adorable puppy one. My dad gave it to me the day we got Dixie, and it looks just like her."

"That's the point," Sammie said. "Everything on this bracelet spells *L-A-U-R-E-N*, and that's the one word Charlie's been trying not to say in there."

"Right," Lauren said. "Evidence. Boy, can I be stupid sometimes."

She dropped the bracelet back in her pocket.

"Listen, Charlie, Brooke said to send you a big hug. Everyone does."

"Lauren, who else knows about this?" I asked her.

She shrugged. "I didn't tell anyone. It's a good thing, too, because Spencer and Lily are on the Honor Board. That would be a bummer if they knew the whole story."

I didn't have the heart to tell her that I was pretty sure one of them did. I wondered what Spencer was saying about me in there.

"Charlie, promise me you'll come find me as soon as you know anything," Lauren said. "They've got to let you stay here. I'll die if they don't. I feel so responsible for this."

"I made my own decision, Lauren. I didn't have to do what I did."

"You're such a good person, Charlie, and I have so much respect for you. Now more than ever. I'm lucky you're my friend."

"You can say that again," Sammie said, a note of sarcasm in her voice.

"For your information, I love your sister," Lauren snapped.

"Yeah, that's why you treat her so well," Sammie snapped back.

"Listen, you guys, this isn't helping," I said. "Let's just all keep our fingers crossed that this turns out okay."

"Are you kidding, Charlie?" Lauren said, squeezing my hand. "I'm keeping everything crossed."

"Then maybe you can hop on away from here," Sammie said. "You don't want this door to open up and have everyone see you."

"Right. Evidence." Lauren gave me one last hug, then quickly headed down the stairs.

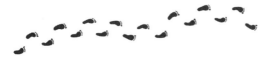

The minutes passed slowly out in the hall. I could hear voices from inside, and they sounded like they were involved in a heated debate. The bell for second period rang, and the hall filled up with kids, but still the voices from inside the conference room continued.

"You should go to class," I said to Sammie. "Who knows how long this will take."

"Right," Sammie said. "I'm leaving. I'll go get some cinnamon rolls and hang with my friends. We'll talk about our party and just have a lot of laughs."

"Really?" I asked.

"Not," she said.

There it was, the old Sammie sarcasm. That's the sister I knew.

Finally, in the middle of second period, the door opened and Phoebe came out.

"We've reached a decision," she said. "You can come in now."

Suddenly, my knees grew weak, and I actually had to grab on to Sammie's arm to keep me upright. None of this had seemed entirely real before. Now that I was about to learn my fate, it was all too real.

"I don't think we need you inside," Phoebe said to Sammie.

"I think we do," she answered. And holding my arm, she brushed past Phoebe and walked into the conference room by my side.

Phoebe took her seat in the brown leather chair and read over some notes on the yellow pad in front of her.

"We had a very hard time coming to a verdict," she began. "The opinion was split down the middle. We had to take several votes. Finally, after much discussion, we came to a final vote on whether or not to expel you. You should know that the vote was three to two."

I thought I was going to throw up. There it was. Obviously, Spencer and Lily had voted to keep me in school, and the three others had voted to expel me. What was going to happen to me now? I had to go to seventh grade somewhere. Would they take me back at Culver City, my old school? Or would I have to go to some kind of special school for kids who had been expelled, if they even have such things? I put my head in my hands.

"It was three to two *in your favor*," Lily said. "You're going to stay, Charlie."

I couldn't believe my ears. Lily's voice sounded like an angel was talking to me.

"Really?" I said. "Oh, thank goodness. Thank you. Thank you."

"Don't thank her," Phoebe said. "You don't know that she voted to keep you. Our vote here is confidential, between us. Therefore, you should thank all of us."

"That's what I meant," I said. "Thank all of you. I am so grateful."

"Me too," Sammie piped up. For the first time in twenty-four hours, she actually had color in her cheeks. I think we both felt like we had been holding our breath for a day.

Principal Pfeiffer cleared his throat. He had put his pen down and was no longer marking up his yellow pad, but he was still rubbing his head.

"You are very lucky, Ms. Diamond," he said, "that your fellow students showed compassion for you. Frankly, I wouldn't have done the same. However, they think a great deal of you and are willing to give you a second chance to prove yourself."

"But there are conditions," Olivia said before I could get too happy. "You're on probation until the end of the semester, and you have all of the following punishments."

"I'll read them," Phoebe interrupted. "I'm chairperson." From the tone of her voice, it was clear to me that she was not one of the people who had voted in my favor.

"First of all," she began. "Your grade on the midterm will be changed to an F. Second of all, you will have one month's detention every day after school. And third of all, you are forbidden to participate in any after-school activities for the rest of the semester. That means you'll have to drop cheerleading, but you would have had to, anyway, because you'll be in detention."

"You forgot the lunch thing," Olivia said to her.

"I'm getting to that," Phoebe snapped. "Three times a week at lunch, you'll have to do community service. We considered assigning you to tutor a sixth-grader, but then Ms. King suggested you work with Luz in the vegetable garden. He feels bad about turning you in, and you have a lot to make up to him."

As bad as the punishment was, I felt like a hundred-pound weight had been lifted off my back.

"The meeting is hereby adjourned," Phoebe said. "I want to thank my fellow members for attempting to maintain impartiality during our adjudication."

Wow. Either Phoebe had been watching too many legal shows on TV or she just had a huge vocabulary. I'd never heard an eighth-grader use so many big words in one sentence. I felt sorry for Will. It would definitely be rough to be a second child living in the shadow of a sister like Phoebe. No wonder he needed Truth Tellers. I would, too.

Sammie and I waited while all the committee members left. Principal Pfeiffer was the first out the door, followed by Lily, who flashed me a relieved smile on her way out.

"That was a close one," Bounce said as he passed by. "But you're tough, you'll be okay."

Olivia and Phoebe said nothing, just pretended that I didn't even exist. Spencer did the same. No smile, no dimple, no acknowledgment that I was even in the room. In fact, as he pushed past me, he looked furious. I could see him clenching his jaw, which changed the whole look of his face. It reminded me of that time a couple weeks before when a careless guy on a bike bumped into me on the bike path and knocked me down.

"You need to watch where you're going, buddy," my dad had said to him, clenching his jaw in just the same way. "You could hurt an innocent person."

As Sammie and I got up to leave, Ms. King approached us. I hoped she wasn't going to give me a lecture. It was the last thing I needed.

"I have a message for your grandmother," she said, lifting her glasses off her face and moving them to the top of her head. "Tell her I think she's a very wise woman. We all have to learn how to forgive ourselves."

She smiled, put her glasses back on, and left before I had a chance to really absorb what she'd said. There would be time for that, though. I had a lot of hours of detention to put in.

Lauren cried when she heard the news that I was staying at Beachside. She wanted me to come to lunch and sit next to her at the SF2 table, but I couldn't. Ms. King had sent me a note during third period saying that I had to arrange my detention schedule and also go find Luz and make plans to work with him every Monday, Wednesday, and Friday.

I found him out in the garden. Beachside has this community garden that's in back of the art building, next to the soccer field. The Garden Club plants vegetables to give to the homeless shelter. Luz was busy pulling weeds from a patch of what looked like red-and-green lettuce leaves.

"I've been assigned to help you," I said, sticking out my hand to show that there were no hard feelings. "I'm Charlie Diamond."

"You look like your sister," he said.

"We're identical," I said. "Well, almost identical."

"I'm sorry I got you in trouble. You seem like a nice girl."

"You didn't get me in trouble. I got myself in trouble."

He just nodded. "There are some extra gloves in the shed," he said. "Go get them and I'll show you how you can tell the weeds from the plants."

Jillian and Brooke came by while I was working with Luz.

"Eeuuww," Jillian said. "You're going to get all filthy in there."

I didn't mind, though. Having my hands in the dirt actually felt kind of good. And Luz let me plant two whole rows of carrots. He called them "Charlie's Carrots," and he said I could take care of them until they were ready to harvest.

It was sixth period that was the killer. History. Mr. Newhart. I ran all the way there so I'd arrive early enough to talk to him in private.

"What do you want, Charlie?" he said when I walked in. He didn't look up from his computer.

My heart was racing. What could I say? "I just want to say how sorry I am," I blurted out.

"I've changed your grade on the midterm," he said, still not looking up. "It brings your average down to a C-minus. You'll have to do a lot of work to catch up. And from now on, the file cabinet will remain locked."

"For what it's worth, I didn't cheat."

"For what it's worth, yes, you did," he said, looking at me straight in my eyes. "History tells us, Charlie, that those who stand by and watch something wrong happen are just as wrong as those who do the wrongful deed. The reason for studying history is to learn from it. I hope you do."

I had been really hoping that he would be nice about everything, tell me that he understood, and that all was forgiven. But he wasn't nice, and when I think about it, he had no reason to be. It was just wishful thinking on my part.

Other kids were starting to file in, and, really, neither of us had anything more to say.

"I'll do better, Mr. Newhart. I'm sorry I disappointed you."

He looked up from his computer. "I told you several days ago, Charlie, that I see exceptional potential in you. Prove me right."

I had my work cut out for me, and I knew it. But I was determined.

I would prove him right. For him. For Sammie. And mostly, for myself.

Facing
the Music

....

Chapter 14

"Hi, girls," GoGo said. "Charlie, a friend of yours just called."

GoGo was standing at the screen door of the Sporty Forty as Sammie and I returned home from school that day. She had gotten her cast off a couple of days before, and she was getting around pretty well on crutches. Ryan was standing next to her, just to be extra cautious in case she needed backup. Of course, GoGo wasn't using just any old crutches. She had glued green and blue rhinestones on hers to make them fancy and wrapped colorful tie-dyed scarves around the two crossbars at the top. She said those scarves put her armpits in a good mood.

"Was it Lauren?" I asked her. "She said she'd call."

"Guess again."

"Spencer?" That was too much to hope for.

"No. Think about it, Charlie. You should be able to guess. It has to do with something that happened in school today."

"Oh, Lily March. Is she at home? Can I call her?"

"It was not Lily," GoGo said. "It was your good friend, Principal Pfeiffer. We had a very informative conversation."

"You're duck meat, Charlie," Ryan said. "You might as well go to your room now, because you're never coming out."

No one laughed. Well, Ryan did, but he's an idiot.

"Come sit with me out on the deck," GoGo said. "Ryan and Sammie, you kids go inside. Charlie and I need a little private face time."

"I want to watch," Ryan said. "This is better than *Dr. Phil* on TV."

"Is everything a joke to you?" Sammie asked, taking him by the arm and yanking him into the living room.

"Where's your sense of humor, Sams?"

"Obviously, not where yours is," Sammie said. "Inside, big guy. Let's get you a box of Cheerios to feed on."

I followed GoGo as she hobbled across the deck to the round redwood umbrella table. She sat down on the cushioned chair, and I adjusted the striped umbrella so the sun didn't hit her directly in the face.

"So," she said, placing her crutches on the deck

beneath her. "Is it true what he said? That you stole a test?"

"Yes. But I didn't steal it for me."

"Does that make it better, Charlie?"

"No, not really."

"I'm not going to ask for whom you stole it," GoGo said, "because I respect the fact that you want to protect a friend. But I hope you realize that no matter how much you love your friends, and I commend you for your loyalty, stealing is never acceptable."

"I made a mistake, GoGo. I know that now."

"People pay for their mistakes," she said. "And your principal was very specific in describing all the various ways you will pay. I'm sure your father will have a few choice additions of his own."

"You're going to tell him?"

"Of course. I have to. Did you think I would keep this a secret from him?"

Actually, I did think that. When it came to protecting us from our parents, GoGo always had our backs. She'd wrangle an extra hour for us until bedtime or sneak flashlights into our room so we could read under the covers or let us eat extra candy on Halloween.

"He doesn't have to know, GoGo. It's not like I'm not being punished."

"He's your father, Charlie."

"I know. But how's it going to help me for him to know?"

"Probably not at all; however, you're missing the point, my darling. I know about what you did. And now that I know, I can't lie to protect you. Haven't you learned anything from your experience? That's exactly what you did with your friend. Lied and stole to protect her. Don't you see? If I protected you from your father, I'd be just as guilty as you are."

"But, GoGo, he's going to be really mad."

"It won't be pleasant, I can assure you of that."

I shuddered at the thought of the confrontation with my dad. He didn't like it when we lost a tennis match. This thing was going to be a major scene.

"Where is he now?" I asked. Maybe there was still time to pack some peanut butter and jelly sandwiches and run away like Claudia did in my all-time favorite book, *From the Mixed-up Files of Mrs. Basil E. Frankweiler.* Of course, Claudia and her brother ran away to the Metropolitan Museum of Art, which is in New York, but maybe I could find a museum in Los Angeles to hide in.

GoGo looked at her watch.

"Let's see. He's on the way back from Santa Barbara. If he beats the traffic, he should be here in about an hour. You'd best prepare yourself, Charlie. Get a snack. You'll need some fortification."

I suddenly realized that I was starving. I hadn't eaten much for dinner the night before, and Sammie and I ran out before breakfast. I skipped lunch to work in the garden with Luz, which meant it had been twenty-four hours since I'd eaten. I left GoGo sitting on the deck and went into the kitchen. Ryan was at the counter, pouring a huge bowl of cereal. He eats cereal out of a mixing bowl, the big one in the stack of three. Sammie had her hand in the cookie jar, which technically she wasn't supposed to do because she's not supposed to eat sugar. Esperanza was putting a pan of chicken into the oven to roast.

"Hola, Charlie," she said with a bright smile.

"Hey, Esperanza," I answered.

"Candido is coming to pick me up. Maybe I tell him to bring Alicia to visit with Sammie. Maybe you could join them. You look so sad."

"Not today, Espie," Ryan said, pouring half the carton of milk into his giant bowl. "There's going to be fireworks here."

"That's good. Alicia, she loves fireworks."

"Not these kind, Espie. Trust me, it's not going to be pretty."

"Ryan, remember to take the chicken out in an hour, or it won't be pretty, either. It will be a very ugly chicken."

"Good one, Espie." Ryan laughed. "Very punny."

She laughed, too. Then she smoothed her dress, took the rubber band out of her hair, and shook her hair loose. Still smiling, she went into the living room to get her things together.

"Alicia looks like her mother," I said to Sammie

as I grabbed a banana and peeled it. "I never noticed before."

"I've been there when Esperanza gets all dressed up to go to church," she said. "She looks really hot."

"Speaking of hot," Ryan chimed in, his mouth full of cereal. "You should have seen your one true love, Spencer Ballard, at lunch today. He was boiling mad."

"About what?"

"Beats me. He was yelling at Sean and Dwayne ... the one you guys so pathetically call the General. Spencer was so mad, the teacher on duty made him pick up his lunch tray and go to another table."

"You didn't overhear anything?" I asked.

"Not much," Ryan answered. "Spencer said Sean and the General took advantage of someone. I couldn't hear who. He said they were no better than bullies. That did it for Sean. I thought he was going to punch Spencer's lights out. Typical seventh-grader stuff. You kids should grow up and act mature like us."

Then he pressed his cereal spoon to his face and balanced it on his nose. Yeah, real mature.

I tried to do everything right before my dad got home. I set the table, put some potatoes in to bake, and basted the chicken. I made a pitcher of lemonade, straightened up the living room, and even watched some of the *Improving Your Tennis Serve* video and took notes. Ryan just sat there on the couch shaking his head as I made everything perfect.

"It's not going to help, Charles. Your goose is cooked."

"I thought you said I was duck meat."

"Whatever kind of poultry you are, dude, you're fried," he said. "Pretty punny, huh?"

Sammie was in our room, talking to Alicia on the phone. Apparently, after the history midterm, Alicia had revved up their party and sent e-vites to all their friends. She and Sammie were going over the list of the kids who had accepted so far. It was all the kids who weren't invited to Ben's bar mitzvah.

Ben's bar mitzvah . . . at least I had that to look forward to. November twenty-third was still three weeks away. It was going to be a tough time. Detention every day after school. No cheerleading practice. Working in the community garden. Reporting in to Ms. King twice a week. Trying to bring up my history grade. Not much fun in any of it. But at least at the end of the month, I'd still get to go to the party of the year. Just the thought made me happy. I felt like Cinderella slaving over her chores while she looked forward to going to the ball. I wished I knew what was going on with my Prince Charming. Maybe his fight with Sean and the General was about defending me. But then, maybe it was about something totally different. You never know with boys.

GoGo was back inside, resting on the couch, when I heard my dad's car pull up in the driveway.

"Time to face the music," she said.

"He's going to kill me."

"You'll live. And remember, darling, that which doesn't kill you makes you stronger."

I know she meant that to be encouraging, but instead it just totally scared me.

My dad was in a great mood when he walked in.

"Smells delicious in here," he said, throwing his blue Sporty Forty windbreaker over the back of the flowered chair. "And it looks great, too. I like it when it's tidy."

"I straightened up, Dad. And there's baked potatoes in the oven."

"Charlie, you're a good girl." He bent down and gave me a kiss on the top of the head.

"Rick," GoGo said, "Charlie has something to say to you."

"Can't it wait until after dinner? I'm starving. I worked three matches today, including one wheelchair tennis match. Bless their hearts, those kids can really move around the court. They're amazingly athletic."

"I'm going to go take a shower," GoGo said to me. "You two talk it out."

Dad gave me a puzzled look and sat down in the flowered chair.

"This sounds serious," he said. "I hope you're not injured. You have tournament matches every other Sunday until Christmas."

"I'm not injured, Dad. And I'm going to work really hard to do well in those matches."

"That's my girl. So then why the long face?"

"I got in some trouble at school today," I began, trying to adopt a casual tone. At first, he didn't look too concerned, but as I proceeded with the story, his eyebrows furrowed and he started to do that clenching thing with his jaw. By the time I got to the Honor Board part, he was on his feet, pacing back and forth. I finished with telling him the verdict and the school consequences, along with a big and heartfelt apology.

I thought he would yell, but he didn't. He was quiet for a long time, which was way worse. He just kept pacing back and forth, back and forth.

"I knew your mother should never have gone away," he said at last. "I knew that without her supervision something terrible like this would happen with you girls."

"It's not Mom's fault," I said. "She didn't do anything. *I* did. *I* made the mistake."

"This is not just a little mistake, Charlie, a minor miscalculation. What you did was make a major error in judgment. The kind of error that makes me doubt everything you do."

Oh, this is worse than I thought.

"I don't know how you expect me to trust you," he went on. "Can you help me with that, Charlie? Can you tell me how you're planning to rebuild my trust in you?"

"I'll do everything right, Dad. I swear. I've learned my lesson. I have to stay after school for detention, but the minute I come home, I'll practice with Sammie. I'll do my chores just like I did today and finish my homework on time. And we'll do really well in the tournaments. I promise, Dad. I'll show you that I'm responsible and that you can trust me."

He listened, just gazing out the window at the waves crashing on the beach, clenching his jaw without even realizing it. I heard a click and saw that the door to our bedroom had opened a crack. On the other side, I could see Sammie and Ryan poking their noses out, listening.

"I'm going to take you at your word, Charlie," he said at last. "I'm going to give you a chance to rebuild my trust, but your behavior cannot go without consequences. You are grounded for the entire month of November. You will go to school and take care of your responsibilities there. You will practice with your sister and focus on your tennis. And if I see that you are doing everything you promise, your life can go back to normal by the end of November."

"By what date at the end of November?" I asked. The words fell out of my mouth before I could stop them.

"I said the end of November. What about that do you not understand?"

"But, Dad," I whined. "Ben Feldman's bar mitzvah is November twenty-third."

"Then I'm afraid Ben Feldman will have to celebrate his bar mitzvah without you."

He stood up and headed into the kitchen. I ran after him.

"You can't do that," I begged him. "Please. You remember, it's not just another party. It's the one at Dodger Stadium. The best party of the year. I can't miss it."

"You should have thought of that earlier," he said. "Before you used such poor judgment."

"But, Dad . . ."

"Do not 'but, Dad' me, Charlie. You brought this on yourself. You've got some things to prove to me. This conversation is over."

He turned and went into the kitchen. I could hear him getting the chicken and potatoes out of the oven. I could hear him, but I couldn't see him very well. That's because my eyes were filled with tears.

I ran into my room and nearly knocked Sammie and Ryan down. I flung myself on the bed sobbing.

"Wow, Charles, I'm really sorry," Ryan said. "That's rough."

"Don't cry," Sammie said, coming over to sit on the edge of my bed. "We'll figure something out. Here, have a tissue."

She picked up the box from our nightstand and held it out to me. As I reached out, I saw what had been tucked away underneath it. It was the invitation to Ben's bar mitzvah, the perfect and amazing midnight-blue passport to fun. Ms. CHARLOTTE JOY DIAMOND, it said in elegant, sparkly letters. I picked it up and looked at it, held it to my nose to smell the salty peanut aroma.

This is where it all had begun.

And this is where it would end, with my big, fat, wet tears falling on the beautiful golden letters.

Grounded

....

Chapter 15

"At least let us bring you a Frappuccino," Lauren said. "It will cheer you up."

It was another rotten Thursday, and I was sitting in Ms. King's conference room serving detention. For the past two weeks, I had spent two after-school days a week there and three days a week with Ms. Pontoon in the library. Although I didn't like any of it, I liked the library days better. At least there was something to do. I helped Ms. Pontoon return the books to the shelves and cleaned off the computer screens and keyboards, which was badly needed because those sixth-graders leave the keys really sticky. I guess that's what happens when you eat red licorice for lunch.

On the days when I went to Ms. King's for detention, there was never much to do. She let me work on homework, but it was really hard to concentrate in there. Two other kids named Chelsea and Anthony had detention for leaving the school grounds at lunch, and all they did was talk nonstop about their weekend plans. I couldn't join in, because of course, I had no weekend plans—unless you consider doing homework, practicing tennis, and watching TV as plans, which I don't.

Lauren always stopped by Ms. King's to visit. Technically, you can't have visitors in detention, but Ms. King wasn't all that strict, and Lauren only stayed for a few minutes.

"Come on, Charlie. Say yes," Lauren said. "Ryan and I could walk over to Starbucks and be back here in ten minutes." She and Ryan had gotten into the habit of going to Starbucks on Thursdays because her cheerleading practice and his volleyball practice got out at the same time.

"You can bring me a peppermint hot chocolate," Anthony piped up.

"Sure, with extra whipped cream," Ryan said. "How about a poppy seed muffin? And maybe some of that yummy lemon pound cake?"

"Yeah, sounds great."

"It was a joke, dude. Where's your sense of humor?"

"I save it for funny things," Anthony answered. He wasn't amused and I didn't blame him. Sitting in after-school detention every day tends to put you in a bad mood.

"Thanks for stopping by, guys," I said to Ryan and Lauren. "I'm okay here."

"Yeah, we have a hot Twenty Questions competition going on," Chelsea added. "It's all kinds of fun."

Lauren slipped into the chair next to me and got that confidential tone in her voice that I love.

"So I talked to Spencer today in science," she whispered. "He asked about you."

"I'm sure he didn't. He's mad at me. He passed by the garden at lunch and said he was checking to see if my carrots had sprouted."

"Oh, the old carrot excuse," Lauren giggled. "Can't you see through that, Charlie? He just wants to talk to you."

"I don't think so, Lauren. He hasn't been the same since the Honor Board thing. Last week, when we happened to be next to each other in the cafeteria line, I asked him if he voted to expel me or keep me in school."

"Of course he voted to keep you, silly. He's one of us."

"He wouldn't say. He said he had promised to keep the vote secret, and he was bound to that promise. Since then, we haven't talked much."

"None of us have talked to you much. You're stuck inside like a hermit. And we all miss you tons. I wish you could come shopping with us this weekend. Jillian and Brooke and I are going to get shoes for Ben's party. My dress is black so I've decided I'm going with silver shoes."

"Silver and black are really cute together," I nodded, trying to sound cheerful. I had done my best to put Ben's party out of my mind, which I was able to do, like, 2 percent of the time. The other 98 percent of the time I was miserable about having to miss it.

"Maybe your dad will change his mind," Lauren said.

"That's not going to happen. He even told my mom all about it, and she's on his side. GoGo, too. Everyone in the family's against me."

"Correction," Ryan, whose big ears had probably overheard our whole conversation, interrupted. "Every *adult* in the family is. Sammie and I are on your side. In fact, we happen to have something in the works to spring you. A prison break."

This got my interest. "What is it?"

"Can't say yet, Charles. It's a top secret plan."

"Really?"

"Yuppo. Let me just say, it involves hiding a file in a cake so you can use it to saw the bars on your room in half and break out when the guards aren't watching. I saw that in a really cool prison movie once."

That's the thing about Ryan. He wants to help. His heart is in the right place. But in the end, the ridiculous side of him wins out, and he turns out to be just a big old goofball.

"I saw that movie, man," Anthony said. "The guy got away and escaped to Mexico."

Anthony put out his arm, and he and Ryan had a major fist bump.

"I've never understood why boys love prison movies," Lauren remarked. "There's no kissing and all those inmates wear such ugly clothes."

"I'm afraid you'll have to discuss that weighty matter at another time," Ms. King said, coming out of her office and pushing her glasses up on top of her head. "This is detention, not a chitchat room. You kids have been here much too long."

Lauren and Ryan said good-bye and hurried out the door. Ms. King went back into her office and closed the door. After two seconds, she stuck her head out and said to me, "By the way, tell her it's all about male bonding."

"Excuse me?"

"Prison movies," she said. "They are the ultimate male-bonding experience. It's a psychological fact."

Then she smiled and closed the door.

My dad had gotten into the habit of picking me up after detention. I know what you're thinking . . . that he felt bad for me and was trying to be nice. But that wasn't what was going on at all. He needed me to get home fast so Sammie and I could get in at least a forty-five-minute workout before sunset. Daylight savings time had ended the first week in November, and it got dark by five o'clock, so my detention had really cut into our practice schedule. We were playing well, though. We had sailed through our first tournament in November at the Malibu Racquet Club, winning both our matches in straight sets. I don't want to say that being grounded was good for my tennis, but there is something to be said for not having any distractions.

"You looking forward to your match on Sunday?" my dad asked as we drove down Arizona Avenue past the promenade. By the way, that's the promenade where I wouldn't be shopping for shoes with my friends.

"At least I get to leave the house," I answered. "That's a major treat these days."

"Well, it's an important tournament. It's a lead-up to the Junior Nationals, and teams from all over the state are coming in. It's a real opportunity for you girls to be seen. It should attract quite a crowd."

"We'll be ready. We can practice all day Saturday."

"Not so fast. Your sister made a plan to go do something with her friends in the afternoon, which I'm not happy about, but she said it was for school so I couldn't say no."

"Ms. Carew arranged for the Truth Tellers to get together with a group from Lincoln and one other school," I said. "They're calling it the Circle of Truth."

"I don't see the fun in that," he said. "Sounds terribly serious. By the way, I ran into Tom Ballard at the club this morning. The city councilman. He was doing some yoga on the beach. I think you girls should do some yoga stretching. It's very good for preventing injuries."

"Spencer's dad?"

"He's a nice guy. Anyway, I told him about the tournament Sunday, and he said he might stop by. There'll be lots of hands to shake, he said. It's tough being a politician. You've got to love people."

I think he yakked on about the qualities it takes to run for public office, but to tell the truth, I had stopped listening. There was only one thought in my mind, the hope that Mr. Ballard would bring his son to the match.

When we got home, Sammie and Ryan and GoGo were waiting for us on the couch, sitting there all lined up like a row of ducks.

"What's this?" Dad asked, tensing up a bit. I have to admit, they did look a little like a firing squad.

"Family meeting," Sammie answered.

"Oh yeah?" he said suspiciously. "What's it about?"

"The subject is prison breaks," Ryan said, winking at me. Yes, he actually winked, and although I hate to admit it, the guy can pull off a wink, a rare quality in a boy.

"Prison breaks. Good subject," my dad nodded. "That would include some of my favorite movies."

Wow, Ms. King sure knew what she was talking about. At the very mention of prison movies, my dad's eyes lit up and his tension seemed to disappear. Whatever this family meeting was about, Ryan had set the scene for it very well.

My dad sat down on the flowered chair, and I perched on the ottoman. Sammie cleared her throat and began.

"I called this meeting to discuss a change of plans," she said. "And I just want to add that Ryan and I are in agreement, so we already have two votes on our side."

"Unfortunately, this family is not a democracy. So let's hear what you have in mind, and your mother and I will make the decision together."

"As you know," Sammie went on, "the Saturday after next I am having my party here. So far, seventeen of my friends are coming. Everyone is really excited about it."

"If the change you're about to suggest is that I not be here to chaperone, you can forget it right now," Dad said.

"Just listen, Dad," Sammie responded. "It has

nothing to do with you. We only want sixteen kids at the party, so we have to eliminate someone. I've gone over the list and decided who to eliminate. Sorry, Charlie, it's you."

"What are you talking about?" I asked her. "I'm only going to be here because I'm grounded and have nowhere else to go."

"That's exactly the point," Ryan said. "You should be with your friends while Sammie is with hers. Let's face it, try as you might, you're just not geek material."

"We're not geeks," Sammie said. "We're explorers on the path of our true selves."

"Same difference," Ryan said.

"What's your point, Sammie?" Dad asked. "I'm starving."

"Ryan and I think Charlie has done such a great job showing that she's sorry that we believe she should be allowed to go to Ben's party," she declared. "That solves both of our problems."

I had to hand it to Sammie. This was a clever approach, one that caught all of us by surprise, even me.

"Also, for your consideration," she went on, "I've gotten all sixteen members of the Truth Tellers to sign this petition in support of Charlie."

She stood up and handed a rolled-up piece of paper to Dad. When he unrolled it, I saw that it was titled FREE CHARLIE! and had a whole bunch of signatures.

My dad looked at me suspiciously.

"Did you put her up to this?"

"I'm totally shocked, Dad." And that was the truth. I had seen Sammie designing something on her computer a couple of nights before, but I had no idea she had put together this whole plan. She was being very brave, because as I think you've probably noticed, our dad is not an easy guy.

"Phyllis?" he said, turning to GoGo. "You're in on this, too?"

"I am not," she answered. "I am only here because I was asked to attend. This is a parental decision. I would never interfere."

"So what do you say, Dad?" Ryan asked. "Can we spring the girl from prison?"

"I'm not inclined to say yes," Dad said. "I set the end of November as the date, and I don't see any reason to change it."

"Then you leave us no choice but to haul out Plan B," Ryan said. Then, switching into his Kermit voice, he said "Hit him with it, Sam-I-Am. Prison Break, Plan B."

"We know how much next Sunday's tournament means to you," Sammie said. "We are determined to be the picture of focus and responsibility. We'll practice every spare minute up until the first match."

"What about the Circle of Truth on Saturday?" I asked her.

"I'm going to stay here and practice with you,"

Sammie said. "I already told Ms. Carew I couldn't go. I have a feeling there will be plenty of other geek fests in my future."

"So, Sam-I-Am, spit out the plan already," Ryan said. "Or I will."

"What we propose, Dad, is this." Sammie stood up as if she were about to make a speech. "If we win, you spring Charlie. She's ungrounded, and she can go to the bar mitzvah. If we lose, I'll cancel my party, and we both stay home. We stand together on this. Two halves of the same circle. Either we both win or we both lose."

I couldn't believe what she was saying. It was an amazing thing she was offering. Even Dad agreed.

"This is very impressive," Dad said.

"You've raised two very excellent girls," GoGo said. "There's a lot of love between them."

Dad nodded, but he didn't say yes.

"Can I assume you've spoken with your mother about this?" he asked Sammie.

"Yup, she said she would support whatever decision you make."

I held my breath as he stood up, wishing on everything I could wish on—rainbows, shooting stars, dandelions, fallen eyelashes. You know the list. Dad paced around for a minute, then came over to Sammie and kissed her on the top of her head. And then he did the same to me.

"I am proud that you two stand up for each other,"

he said. "Now I want you to prove yourselves."

"Does this mean it's a deal?" Sammie said.

"No, it simply means that you have to prove yourself. I will make a fair decision when the time comes."

"But we want a decision now!" Sammie said.

"That's not the way justice works, Sammie. I will consider all the facts at the appropriate time, and I can promise you, I will make the most fair decision I can."

With that, Dad left and went into the kitchen to take the chicken out of the oven.

"Well," Sammie said, throwing her arms around me. "That's better than nothing." We stood there, hoping and wishing and hugging like bears.

"Hey, what about me?" Ryan said, throwing his long arms around both of us. "How about a little love for the brother?"

Don't worry. We let him in on the hug. Despite being an idiot and a moron and a goofball, he's a good guy.

In two minutes, Sammie and I had changed into our tennis clothes and were out on the court. As we bent over to do our stretching exercises, a routine we had done so often that we moved like we were one person instead of two, Sammie whispered to me, "We can do this, Charlie."

"You're the best, Sammie," I whispered back to her.

And I meant it with all my heart. What a sister. What a friend. Forget male bonding. Female bonding rocks!

The Matchup

....

Chapter 16

"Are you nervous?" Sammie asked as we headed onto the court for our first match the following Sunday.

"I won't lie," I said. "I have a few butterflies."

It had rained the night before, and the tournament was starting a little late because they had to squeegee off the courts to make sure they were dry. Playing on a wet and slippery surface can be dangerous, and the officials had to be careful to protect the players.

Sammie and I didn't know any of our opponents because they were all from Northern California. That meant we had no idea what to expect, competition-wise. The two girls who were walking onto the court certainly had a size advantage. They looked like they were sixteen, even though I knew they weren't because you have to show your birth certificate when you sign up for your age category. In any case, their arm muscles were bigger than my leg muscles. That wasn't exactly a confidence builder.

"We can take them," Sammie said as she unzipped her racket case.

"No distractions," I agreed.

"Not even if Spencer shows up with his dad."

"Not even then."

We shook hands with the muscle women. They had what I'd call a killer grip.

We were serving first. Specifically, I was serving first. Sammie could tell I was shaky. After all, I had a lot to prove to our dad on this day. So before I served, she came up to me with some final words of advice.

"Here's what you have to do, Charlie. Visualize what's motivating you to win. Like a giant trophy. Or the awards ceremony and how great that will feel. Keep that image in your head at all times. It will keep you focused."

I took her advice, but what I visualized had nothing to do with a trophy or an awards ceremony. The picture I painted in my head was of me dancing with Spencer Ballard at Ben's party. The music was slow, and he had his hands on my waist. He was holding me and singing softly along with the music. He held me tight and twirled me around the floor.

With that perfect image in my head, I threw the ball up in the air and came down on it hard. *Smash.* It was an ace. From the stands, I could hear Ryan yelling, "You go, Charles!" You're not supposed to cheer at tennis matches, but self-control isn't exactly one of Ryan's strong points.

I hate to brag, but my next serve was even better. I had a rhythm going, which is crucial in a tennis serve. It's all about rhythm. I'd toss the ball in the air, visualize dancing with Spencer, and hit a perfect shot across the net. I kept it up through the whole match. *Toss, Spencer, perfection. Toss, Spencer, perfection.*

The muscle girls were strong but not fast. They couldn't get a racket on my serve. Sammie played like a dynamo, too. She covered the back court and returned everything they hit at her. She's not usually fast, but that day, her feet were moving like a tap dancer's. I wondered what she was visualizing that got her to focus like that. Knowing Sammie, it was probably s'mores.

We won in two sets, 6–2 and 6–2. Our dad was over the moon.

"You girls played like champions," he said, running onto the court when the match was over. "We should have that 'prove yourself' talk before every match."

In some tournaments, we play three matches a day, but because of the late start and the rain, there was only going to be time for two today, which raised an ugly question.

"So, Dad," I asked when we went into the

clubhouse to drink some vitaminwater. "If we lose the next match, then we'll be one and one for the day."

"And your point is, Charlie?"

"My point is, will we have proven ourselves well enough for our deal? Do you consider that a win?"

"Since when is a tie a win?" he said. "Unless they've changed the rules when I wasn't looking, a tie is a tie."

"That's not fair," Sammie said. "If we lose the next match, no parties?"

Dad just shrugged. "I haven't made any promises," he said. "I am reserving judgment. However, the best solution to your dilemma is simple, girls. Don't lose the next match."

Easier said than done. The team we were playing was from the Rio del Oro Racquet Club in Sacramento, and they trained with one of the top instructors in the Junior Tennis Academy there. Sammie and I had watched them warm up that morning, and they were very slick players. Not huge in size like the previous girls, but smooth and fast and smart. Dad calls it strategic tennis, which means they don't run around a lot, they just happen to be wherever the ball is.

While we were waiting for our names to be called, Sammie went off to the bathroom for the millionth time that day. She pees like a fish when she gets nervous. Actually, I don't think fish pee, so I take that back. Maybe I just should have said she pees a lot when she gets nervous. While I was waiting for her to return, Lauren arrived. She was carrying a big shopping bag from Attitudes, my favorite shop at the mall.

"I'm so sorry I missed your first match," she said. "My mom had a hair appointment and couldn't drive me until now. Ryan texted me that you guys were dynamite."

"Just one more match to go," I said. "Keep your fingers crossed."

"Are you kidding? I've got everything crossed!"

I had told Lauren about the conversation with my dad, and when she heard there was a possibility that I could go to Ben's party, she actually screamed so loud her dad thought she had fallen down the stairs in their house.

Lauren put the Attitudes bag in my lap.

"This is for you," she said. "I bought it weeks ago. To say thank you for . . . you know . . . for that thing you did."

I looked in the bag. Inside was an adorable little red dress. It had a silver zipper going all the way up the front and silver studs around the neckline.

"It'll be perfect for the party," she giggled. "I'll help you find some silver shoes. All you have to do is win a little old tennis match."

It was a great dress. By far, the nicest dress I'd ever had. We don't have much money these days, and Sammie and I got our clothes budget slashed pretty seriously. But I knew I couldn't take it. I put the dress back in the bag and handed it to Lauren.

"This is so sweet of you," I told her. "But I have to give it back."

"I want you to have it, Charlie. After all you've been through for me."

"Lauren, I can't take a present for stealing that test. I'm not proud of what I did. And every time I'd wear that dress, I'd remember the one thing I want to forget."

I could tell she felt bad.

"I hope you understand, Lauren."

"I do. At least, I think I do."

I saw Sammie coming back from the bathroom, so I quickly stuffed the bag under Lauren's chair. I didn't want to have to get into it with Sammie. Besides, I was prepared for her to be rude to Lauren as she had done so often in the past. She's never liked it when Lauren shows up for our tournaments. But Sammie Diamond is a girl of many surprises.

"Thanks for coming, Lauren," she said. She wasn't exactly gushing with enthusiasm but she wasn't totally rude, either. Then she flopped down in one of the big leather chairs in the clubhouse and put her earbuds in. Listening to music is one of the ways she gets her game face on.

And speaking of faces, another excellent one showed up a few minutes later. I'll give you a clue. It has a major dimple on one cheek and is surrounded by blond, curly hair.

"Hi," Spencer said, walking up to me with a basket of sweet potato fries. "Want one?"

"Thanks, but I couldn't. There's a whole swarm of butterflies flapping around in my stomach right now."

"Big match with a lot riding on it." He nodded.

"You know about the conversation with my dad?"

"Lauren told me."

"Listen, Spencer," I began, trying to find the right words. "I know you must think I'm a real creep."

"No, I think you got taken advantage of. And I told those guys so, flat out."

"Thanks for sticking up for me. Anyway, I just want to say that I'm sorry for what I did. It was a mistake."

"I've made mistakes, too." Then he smiled and that dimple popped out. "But never a doozy like that one. You don't do anything halfway, do you?"

He laughed and I laughed.

"That's me. Charlie Diamond. Major-league screwup."

"Yeah, you got one strike against you. But you're not out until you get three strikes, which means you've got two more chances with me."

His voice sounded like the old Spencer, the one on the patch of grass that day at lunch when he gave me one of his granola bars. Soft and sweet.

"I've thought a lot about what happened, Charlie," he said. "You didn't take that test because you're bad. You did it because you have a good heart. It just got in your way, that's all."

He reached out and touched my hand and that swarm of butterflies in my stomach turned into a flock. Sammie pulled her earbuds out and stood up from her chair.

"Hey," she said, flicking his hand away from mine. "None of that. This girl has to focus. A lot of us geeks are counting on her."

"A lot of us non-geeks are, too," he laughed. He didn't say it in a judgmental way. It was nice. Even Sammie laughed.

"Come on, Charles," she said, yanking me away from him. "We're up in a few minutes. You've got to practice your visualization exercise."

It wasn't hard because that image was exactly what I wanted to think about, anyway. His hand on my waist as we twirled around in time to the music.

Toss, Spencer, love. Toss, Spencer, love. Toss, Spencer, love.

It must have worked, because we won the first set. It was close, not nearly as easy as beating the muscle girls, but Sammie and I worked well together and communicated and concentrated, and we squeaked out a 7–5 victory. One more set to go, and we'd both be on our way to party central.

But the team from Rio del Oro Racquet Club wasn't giving up so easily. They'd win one game, and then we'd win one. It went on like that until the game score was 6–6, and the officials declared a twelve-point tiebreaker. Whoever is ahead wins, except the tricky part is you have to win by two points. Sammie and I once played a tiebreaker that went on for over thirty points.

We started the tiebreaker and fought hard for every single point. But so did they. It was 1–1, 2–2, 3–3, and before we knew it, we were tied at 6–6. We got the next point, which meant we were up by one, 7–6. If we could clinch the next point, we'd win. It was their serve, and Sammie was receiving. It was a tough serve to return, and Sammie had to run really fast to get it. As she reached for the ball, her foot slipped out from under her and she fell. From the corner of my eye, I could see our dad jump to his feet in the stands. I raced over and put out my hand to help her up, but she just stayed on the ground, clutching her ankle.

"Are you hurt?" I asked her.

"I hit a slippery patch and totally lost my footing. I'm so sorry, Charlie."

"Is it bad?"

"My ankle," she said. "I really twisted it bad."

The official came, and we helped Sammie hobble to the bench. She could barely stand on her foot. They called a trainer, who took a look at her ankle.

"It's not broken," the official said. "The trainer can wrap it and you can continue, or you can retire from the game. If that's your choice, the match goes to your opponents. We'll take a treatment break, and you'll have ten minutes to decide."

During the break, the trainer wrapped her ankle with tape while I got her some water. I could see our dad pacing back and forth in the aisle. Parents aren't allowed on the court until the match is over.

"How's that feel?" the trainer asked when he had finished.

"Better," she said, but I could tell she was lying. Her face was so twisted in pain that the freckle above her eyebrow was practically sitting on her nose.

"Sammie, you can't play on that ankle," I told her.

"I know," she whispered. "But I can stand on it. You're going to have to do the playing for both of us. A lot of my friends are counting on you."

"Are you sure about this?"

"What choice do we have?"

Sammie leaned on me as she limped back onto the court, and everyone in the stands applauded. The officials took their places, called out the score of 7-7, and the game resumed.

The next serve was to me, and I returned it fine. But our opponents knew Sammie was injured and directed their return shot right to her. There was no way she could hit it back—she'd be lucky just to be able to move out of the way. I flew into action and ran across the court, getting there just in time to return the ball. Their next shot went to the opposite side of the court. I charged as fast as I could and barely got a backhand on it. But I got it over. They kept up the same pattern, hitting it from one side of the court to the other, making me chase the ball back and forth. Sammie was basically out of commission, and every return was up to me. They just kept pummeling me, and I got completely out of breath and felt my calf muscle cramping up.

Keep going, I told myself. *A lot of people are counting on you. Prove yourself.*

And I did. Somehow, I reached into a deep pocket of strength I didn't know I had and returned every shot that was hit to us. Finally, when I thought I couldn't go on, I managed to hit a winner, a long, hard forehand to the baseline. They didn't make it there in time, and the point was ours.

Finally. It was 8–7. One last point to go.

It was my serve. These girls were good at returning serves, so I knew I had to hit a winner. I didn't have the strength left for another long rally like the last one. It was now or never. I took my place at the baseline and bounced the ball a couple of times to settle my nerves.

"Visualize," Sammie called to me. "Focus."

And I did.

Toss, Spencer, love. Toss, Spencer, love.

I didn't see the serve, but I heard it zinging off the sweet spot of my racket and exploding over the net. It was like the stars and the moon had aligned just right.

It was an ace.

We won.

The Surprise

....

Chapter 17

"No way," I proclaimed emphatically, looking at myself in the full-length mirror. "I refuse to wear this. I look like a ten-year-old."

It was six o'clock that evening. Sammie and I had come home after the tennis match to shower and clean up. Dad just dropped us off in front of the club and hurried on to a dinner engagement he had made with Councilman Ballard, Spencer's dad. They were going to talk about getting a permit to build one more tennis court at the Sporty Forty, and the club owners wanted my dad to represent them. In the car, Sammie and I tried to bring up the subject of Ben's bar mitzvah and her party, but he said we'd go into it in detail after he got home. We both just knew he was going to say yes, so after we cleaned up, we started to work on our outfits.

I was standing in my room in a horrible green dress, making faces at myself in the mirror. Sammie had spent the previous hour putting together the outfit she was going to wear to her party. Since it was a costume party, she decided to go as the queen of the hippies. GoGo tried to explain to her that hippies didn't have queens, but she didn't care.

"I just want to look fantabulous," she said.

GoGo had gotten together some of her old clothes from the sixties. Sammie picked out a brown suede vest with flowers and beads sewn all over it, an orange gypsy skirt with purple ruffles and matching headband, and a pair of Native American moccasin boots with fringe. She liked those because they covered up the brace she had to wear for her sprained ankle. The finishing touches to her costume were round wire-rimmed sunglasses with pink lenses and dangly earrings made of feathers.

"I can't believe you actually wore all that stuff," I said to GoGo as I watched Sammie try everything on.

"I not only wore it, my darling, I had a fabulous time in it," GoGo explained. "Sitting around reciting poetry, strumming the guitar, protesting injustice . . . it was a grand era. I'm sorry you kids won't get to experience it."

"We recite poetry in Truth Tellers," Sammie said. "We protest injustice, too. And Bernard is a singer-songwriter. He brought his guitar once."

"Well, then, perhaps you are the hippies of your era," GoGo said.

"Not me," I declared. "Give me a mall and a Frappuccino any day."

"We're all individuals." GoGo reached out and smoothed my hair. "That's what makes the human race so interesting. How sad it would be if we were all the same."

The green dress was the one I wore to my sixth-grade graduation party in June. GoGo said she thought it would be fine to wear to the bar mitzvah since none of the kids at Beachside had seen it, and besides, it had a big, swishy skirt that was just made for dancing. I had gotten Ryan, with his long arms, to reach into the cabinets above our closet and pull down the dress. I slipped it over my head and smoothed it over my hips.

It was November, and the last time I had worn that dress was in June. Funny, I never thought about how much my body had changed in those five months. But as I stared at myself in the mirror, all I could think about was how much I looked like a ten-year-old.

"It is a little snug in the bodice," GoGo said, cocking her head to one side and staring me up and down.

"It flattens out your boobs," Sammie said.

"Which don't exactly need any more flattening," I commented. "And look at this skirt. I never realized how poofy it is. It's like a flower girl's dress at some stupid wedding."

"You could always wear jeans and borrow one of Ryan's baseball jerseys," Sammie suggested. "I mean, the party is at Dodger Stadium."

I picked up the blue-and-gold invitation and read it to Sammie. "'The celebration continues in the clubhouse with an all-star party,'" I read.

"That is definitely not a jeans-and-baseball-jersey kind of affair," GoGo said. "Maybe we can go to the dressmaker and have her let out the bodice some."

"Oh, this is just great." I sighed. "I'm finally getting to go to the party, and I'm going to look like a ten-year-old flower girl." I was trying not to get too upset since I felt lucky to be going to the party at all. But really, the sad truth was, I was going to be the worst-dressed girl there by a mile.

Sammie left the room while GoGo fussed with my dress. She looked inside to see if there was enough material to let it out, and there was. At least that was something. Maybe I wouldn't have totally flat boobs.

"Not to panic." GoGo forced herself to smile. "We'll have your father take you to my dressmaker, Yolanda. She's a wonderful Hungarian woman, and she can fix anything."

Sammie came back in with a big smile on her face.

"I have just put Plan B into effect," she said. "I'd appreciate it if from now on you would please refer to me as Ms. Plan B. Or maybe Madam Plan B. That sounds even better."

"What'd you do?"

"Placed a few strategic phone calls," she said. "I mean, what's the point of having the SF2 girls as your friends if you can't borrow their clothes?"

"You called them?"

"Yup. Lauren and Jillian and Brooke are on their way over. Lily, too. Her mom is picking them all up."

"Say thank you to your sister," GoGo told me.

"Make that thank you, Madam Plan B." Sammie laughed.

The girls arrived fifteen minutes later with armloads of clothes. Lily took charge immediately and had me try on one thing after another.

A spaghetti-strap, turquoise minidress from Brooke.

"Too sexy," GoGo said. "Take it off."

A one-shoulder, purple chiffon dress from Jillian.

"Too Kardashian," Lauren said. "She's so yesterday."

A strapless, brown velvet sheath from Lauren.

"You don't have the boobs for that," Brooke said. "It'll fall down."

A vintage, bohemian maxi-dress from Lily.

"Only Lily can pull off that look," Jillian said. "You'll look ridiculous."

Nothing was exactly right until GoGo came up with an idea.

"Why don't you wear something from each of your friends," she said. "Build your own look."

"What a great idea, GoGo," Lauren said. "Charlie's grandma is just the best."

"Hello . . . she's my grandma, too," Sammie chimed in. "Remember me?"

"Of course we do, Sammie," Lauren said, not even looking in her direction. "Now come on, girls, let's focus."

Everyone helped pick out things for me, but most of the decisions were Lily's. She's like a wizard with clothes. She started with a black velvet miniskirt from Lauren and a red sequined tank from Jillian. Then she put a flouncy, sheer, black peasant top from Brooke over that and gave it shape with her vintage leopard-skin belt loosely draped around my waist. And to finish it off, she loaned me her leopard-skin ballerina flats that tied with black satin ribbons around the ankles.

"There," she said, stepping back to admire me. "What do you think?"

"I think she looks positively radiant," GoGo said. I couldn't have said it better myself. I felt like I was actually glowing.

I twirled around and around, looking at myself in the mirror. All I could do was giggle like an idiot. It was a totally new me!

Sammie had been watching my makeover from her bed.

"What do you think?" I asked her.

"Fantabulous." She nodded. "And I don't use that word lightly."

The girls gathered up their stuff and climbed back into Lily's mom's car. It had taken less than an hour for my total makeover. I didn't even have time to take off my new outfit when I heard Dad's car pull up in the driveway.

"This is so great," I said to Sammie. "He'll get to see me all dressed up so he'll feel really good about saying yes. This is turning out to be so perfect."

I could hear Dad come inside and toss his keys on the green wooden cabinet next to the door. Sammie and I ran out to meet him.

"You like?" I asked, twirling around to show off my new look.

"Sit down, girls," he said, barely noticing what I was wearing. Ryan had crept out from his room and also took a seat on the couch. I was glad. I wanted him there to hear the good news since he had been a part of formulating my rescue plan with Sammie.

"I've come to a decision," Dad began, and I could feel my heart thumping in my chest. I closed my eyes and waited for him to say yes. Would he say it fast, or would he drag it out with a little lecture first? He chose the lecture way.

"Charlie, I hope you know that what you did reflects a serious error in judgment. Stealing is wrong, and there is never an explanation good enough to justify it," he said, speaking slowly and deliberately. "I admire how you've taken your punishment seriously and tried to redeem yourself with excellent discipline in your tennis game."

Okay, Dad, I thought. *Enough of the lecture. Get to the good part.*

"However, after careful consideration and a long conversation with your mother, we have decided that you must adhere to the original punishment. I'm sorry to say, Charlie, that you are still grounded for the remainder of the month."

No! Was this for real? Was I truly hearing this?

"But, Dad," Sammie cried. "You promised."

"I promised to make a fair decision," he said. "And I have not made this decision lightly. I would be a bad father if I let you off the hook for what you did, Charlie. Wrong is wrong is wrong. You have to learn that, and it's up to me to teach it to you."

"Wow, Dad, this is harsh," Ryan said.

But GoGo reached over and took his arm, holding a finger up to her lips to quiet him.

"I'm sure this is difficult for your father," she whispered. "You don't need to make it any more so."

"Fine," Sammie said, standing up defiantly. "Then

if Charlie doesn't get to go to Ben's bar mitzvah, I'm not having my party, either. We stand together on this."

"The final decision is yours," Dad said to her, "but I see no reason for you to punish yourself. You didn't do anything wrong, Sammie. In fact, you have defended your sister with great commitment, and I respect you for that."

I looked down at myself, all dressed up in my new outfit. My eyes filled with tears, just thinking about how no one would see the new me. They would all be out looking their best and laughing, and where would I be? In my room. There was nothing more I wanted than to go to Ben's party, to be part of my new group, to dance with Spencer and feel his arms around me.

Well, there was one thing I wanted more. And that was for my sister to have the good time she deserved.

"You should have your party, Sammie," I said, swallowing my tears. "You deserve it. You guys all deserve it. I'll get over this. There will be other parties."

"Not at Dodger Stadium," Ryan said in his usual sensitive manner. "Those don't come along every day."

He could see my face twist up with emotion.

"Oh, sorry, Charles," he said. "I was sort of an idiot to say that."

Dad got up and went to take a shower. GoGo put her arms around me and held me while I cried. Ryan tried to cheer me up with his Kermit voice. Sammie told me I was still the best sister ever.

Later, Dad came out and heated me up some chicken noodle soup and made grilled cheese. Then the five of us played a game of Scrabble, and Ryan let me win.

It certainly was no party at Dodger Stadium, that was for sure. But it wasn't altogether horrible, either.

The Party

....

Chapter 18

"I feel so awful for you," Lauren said. It was the night of Ben's party, and she had come over to pick up Ryan. She was wearing a totally fabulous black dress and silver shoes, and she looked like she had just stepped out of a major fashion magazine. I, on the other hand, was wearing a pair of gray sweats and a green T-shirt with matching fuzzy green socks. There was no need to put on shoes. I wasn't going anywhere.

"I'll get over it," I said to her, putting on a smile. "Say hi to everyone there."

"Maybe I'll leave early and come by to tell you all about it," she said.

"That'd be really nice, Lauren. I'm dying to hear about it."

Ryan came out of his room, all dressed up in a navy-blue blazer and gray pants. I have to admit, when the guy puts a little effort into it, he can be pretty good-looking. He had added a Dodger cap to his outfit, worn backward with the bill covering his neck. Of course, Ryan being Ryan, he can never do things the ordinary way.

Before they left, Sammie came out of her room, all dressed in her crazy queen of the hippies costume. I had talked her into having the party after all, and finally, she agreed, since all the Truth Tellers had already made plans and were counting on it.

She looked pretty wild, like an authentic hippie with her fringed moccasins and tie-dyed skirt and pink-tinted glasses. We looked at each other and burst out laughing.

"Hey, didn't you guys used to be identical?" Ryan said.

"Almost identical," we both said at once.

A horn honked outside in the driveway.

"Sounds like Chip Wadsworth is getting impatient," my dad called from the kitchen.

"Have the best party ever," I said to Lauren, giving her a hug. "Tell me everything."

"I promise," she said. "We'll take notes, won't we, Ryan?"

Then, placing her hand in his, she waltzed happily out the door.

I wasn't even allowed to go to Sammie's party.

Esperanza had come over to help with the barbecue for the kids, and I got elected to stay in our room with Ramon. Let me put it this way: The highlight of our evening was when he didn't throw up the box of raisins he ate. There was a lot of Candy Land played, interspersed with my tying a cape on him and having him jump on the bed like Superman. Every now and then, I'd let myself think of Dodger Stadium and the great time all my friends were having, and then I'd make myself plaster on a smile and start a pillow fight with Ramon.

From the living room, it sounded like Sammie and her friends were having fun. A couple of times I stuck my head out the door and saw them dancing in their costumes. They are a weird bunch, especially when they dance. No one was doing any steps that you could recognize. They were just out there freestyling in their own goofy ways. And leading the crowd was my sister, the queen of the hippies.

At about ten o'clock, there was a knock on my bedroom door. I thought it would be my dad, coming to ask me to help clean up. After all, isn't that what Cinderella is supposed to do? But it wasn't Dad. It was Sammie.

"Psssst," she whispered. "Someone's here to see you. Waiting on the beach."

"Lauren?" I asked, my heart leaping a little in my chest. She was a good friend and had left the party early to come tell me about it, just like she promised.

"We're going to cover for you," Sammie said. "Alicia said she'd watch Ramon, and I'm going to distract Dad so you can sneak outside. You have exactly ten minutes before you turn into a pumpkin. Don't be late."

"You're the best," I said.

Alicia took over the Superman duty with Ramon, Sammie went to ask Dad to get some graham crackers out of the kitchen for another batch of s'mores, and I threw on my navy-blue hoodie and headed out to the beach. The sand felt cold on my feet, even though I was wearing those ratty, fuzzy green socks, and I shivered a little.

"Lauren?" I whispered. "Where are you?"

I wandered out beyond the deck, away from the fire pit where Sammie's friends were roasting marshmallows. Someone, probably her friend Bernard, was playing the guitar and singing some weird song. I had no doubt that he wrote it, because it sounded so bad. I shook my head and wondered what it was Sammie saw in most of those kids. I hoped Lauren wasn't listening to them. She already thought Sammie was strange, but this would totally convince her.

I squinted into the darkness and noticed someone down by the waves, carrying a little purple glow stick like they give out at fancy dance parties. It gave just enough light to reveal the shape of a person, but not enough for me to see the face.

"There you are," I called to her. "I can hardly see you."

"Well, I can see you," a voice said, "and you're looking good."

It wasn't Lauren's voice. It was Spencer. He came jogging up to me, took the purple tube, and wrapped it around me like a necklace.

"What are you doing here?" I asked him.

"They were giving these out at the party," he said. "I thought you should have one."

"You came all the way here to give me this?"

"I came all the way here to see you. Besides, I was done with the party. It wasn't as much fun without you, so I called my dad to come get me. He's waiting outside for a sec."

"Lauren's coming over, too?" I asked.

"Uh, I wouldn't count on that. Last I saw her, she was dancing with your brother. She didn't look like she was going anywhere."

"It was really nice of you to come over, Spencer."

"I wanted to bring you something."

"The necklace?" I laughed. Even though it cost two cents, it felt like the most beautiful necklace any girl could ever get.

"Yes, the necklace. And I have one more thing for you, if it's okay."

"Sure. What is it?"

"This."

And then he reached out and put his hands on my waist and pulled me close to him. It was dark, but there was just enough glow from my necklace to see that his lips were slightly trembling as he leaned down to kiss me.

And there, on the beach with Bernard's weird music playing in the background and me in my hoodie and fuzzy green socks, I had my first kiss. It wasn't like I imagined it would be. It was better. There was no Dodger Stadium with fireworks going off, no fancy dress or cool deejay. Just me and Spencer and the stars peeking out from under a cloudy California sky.

I had always promised Sammie that I would tell her every detail of my first kiss. But you know what? There are some things a girl just has to keep to herself.

Here's a sneak peek at the next book in the Almost Identical series, Double-Crossed.

....

"The new boys are here!" my twin sister, Charlie, shouted as I jogged across the beach to the lounge chair where she was sprawled out sipping a strawberry smoothie.

Before you get the wrong impression of me, let me tell you right away that I am not a major jogger. In fact, the only thing I hate more than jogging is running. And the only thing I hate more than running is running fast. I think you get the point. But my dad has me on a shape-up program for our next tennis tournament, and if I take a daily run, he lets me eat french fries on the weekend. I'd say that's worth a twenty-minute jog.

"What boys are you talking about?" I asked, grabbing the smoothie from Charlie's hand and taking a giant slurp. "Ouch. Brain freeze."

"Press your thumb against the roof of your mouth," Charlie suggested.

"Why? So I can look stupid?"

"Because it warms up your mouth which gets rid of the brain freeze. Honestly, Sammie, everyone knows that."

I shrugged, but did it, anyway, and after

about twenty seconds, the brain freeze went away. Unfortunately, what didn't go away was our brother, Ryan, who was hanging out on the deck juggling a volleyball in his hands. He dropped the ball, reached into his pocket to pull out his phone, and snapped a picture of me.

"Nice thumb-sucking," he commented, checking out my image on the screen. "Oh, and just a little heads-up, Sammie. That's not a real popular look in the seventh grade."

"Delete it, Ry," I ordered.

"I was thinking that whoever these new boys are might enjoy seeing it. What's it worth to you for me to delete it?"

I lunged for his phone, but he held it up high above his head where I couldn't reach it. The higher Ryan held his phone, the more I jumped, mostly just to harass him. Eventually, it worked.

"Okay, okay, I'll get rid of it," he said. "On one condition: You tell me who these new boys are. Spill it. Could our little Sam-I-Am be having a hot romance?"

"I don't know what you're talking about, Ryan. I don't know any new boys. I barely know any old boys."

"Well, I know who they are," Charlie said. "Their names are Eddie and Oscar."

I just stared at her blankly. None of this was ringing a bell.

"Alicia called when you were jogging," Charlie continued. "Or what you laughingly call jogging because it looks more like creeping. Anyway, she said to tell you her cousins Eddie and Oscar have arrived and she wants to bring them over to say hi."

Ding, ding, ding. A bell rang inside my head. I remembered that when I walked Alicia to her bus stop after school last week, she had mentioned that her twin cousins were coming to visit Los Angeles from El Salvador.

"Listen, Sammie," Charlie said, and from the tone of her voice I knew she was annoyed. "I'm having a little get-together here at the club and it's just for my friends. So maybe you could show Eddie and Oscar to the door, like, pretty immediately after they arrive."

"You're having a party?" I asked Charlie. "What for?"

"It's Saturday," Ryan chimed in. "That's party day for Charlie's friends. Oh, I forgot. So are Monday, Tuesday, Wednesday, Thursday, and Friday. And Sunday."

"It's not really a party," Charlie said. "It's more of a photo shoot."

"A photo shoot!" Ryan laughed. "Just because you girls stand around taking pictures of yourselves trying to look like models does not make it a photo shoot."

"For your information," Charlie said, "we are having an actual fashion photographer here. Lauren has arranged it all."

That shut Ryan up. Lauren Wadsworth, his

sometimes girlfriend, who is rich and beautiful and popular and perfect, probably had her dad call up Seventeen and send over their best photographer.

Charlie got up from her beach lounger and gathered up her headband, sunglasses, and sunscreen from the side table.

"Everybody's going to be here in half an hour," she said to me. "So unless Alicia's cousins are male models, I don't think they'll exactly fit in. Sorry, Sammie. I have dibs on the deck and patio."

Charlie headed down the wooden path to the clubhouse and went into our apartment, letting the screen door slam behind her. I looked over at Ryan and shook my head.

"You've got to give her credit," he said. "That girl is going places in the world. You and me, Sams, we're just ordinary folk."

"I am not ordinary," I snapped, "and you're not either, Ry. You're the captain of the all-city volleyball team and I'm . . . I'm . . ."

"Sweaty," he said, tossing me his terry wrist guard. "You might want to dab your upper lip." Then he headed back out to the beach, tossing the volleyball in the air and setting it with his fingertips as he went.

When I went in the house and checked myself in the bathroom mirror, I discovered Ryan was right. I was a sweaty mess. I took a fast shower, threw on some shorts and a baggy, old, yellow T-shirt, and pulled my hair into a ponytail. When I came out of the bathroom,

Charlie was still trying on outfits, figuring out what to wear to the photo shoot.

"Don't wear white," I said. "Makes you look ten pounds heavier."

"Then I'll look just like you," she answered, and no sooner were the words out of her mouth than she let out a little gasp. "Oh, I didn't mean it to come out that way, Sammie."

"That's okay," I said, even though it actually wasn't. "A fact is a fact. I weigh ten pounds more than you." Actually, that fact wasn't a fact, either, because I weigh twenty pounds more than Charlie.

"Doodle," I heard GoGo call from the kitchen. "Alicia's here."

I ran out of our tiny bedroom, across the tiny living room, and into the tiny kitchen, all in about ten steps. Alicia was waiting for me at the kitchen counter, munching on some taco chips that GoGo was putting on a dip plate.

"Hi," I said, giving Alicia a hug. "So where are these boys everyone's talking about?"

"They're on their way in," she answered. "Oscar's kind of a slowpoke. Wait until you meet them, Sammie. They're so cute. And they're identical, just like you and Charlie."

"Wait . . . I won't even be able to tell them apart?"

"Oh no, you'll totally be able to tell them apart, trust me."

That was a strange thing to say, but before I could

ask what she meant by that, I saw Candido coming in from the parking lot, followed by a boy of about thirteen. He had long, jet-black hair that flopped casually over one eye and the whitest teeth I had ever seen. Alicia had lied—he wasn't cute, he was awesomely gorgeous.

"This is my nephew Eddie," Candido said. Eddie walked right up to me and stuck his hand out. He didn't seem shy in the least.

"Hola," he said.

"Does he speak English?" I asked.

"Sí, I do," he said, and immediately I felt like a total idiot for not asking him directly. "My uncle and my cousin Alicia teach me every summer when they come to visit my country."

He smiled at me with those gorgeous glistening white chompers, and I suddenly wished I had put on a better T-shirt.

If Eddie was this handsome, I couldn't wait to meet his brother. Two of a good thing makes it doubly good. I didn't have long to wait. Oscar came in from the parking lot wearing a blue and white soccer jersey. He had the same shiny black hair as his brother, the same sparkling teeth, the same adorable smile. But there was one major difference. Something was wrong with his leg. A major something.